P9-EDQ-284

A Part for
Addie

A Part for
Addie

JANET O'DANIEL

Houghton Mifflin Company Boston 1974

Library of Congress Cataloging in Publication Data

O'Daniel, Janet, 1921–
   A part for Addie.

   SUMMARY: In the late 1880's two determined sisters interrupt their
theatrical career to uncover a murder plot against their grandfather.
   [1. Mystery and detective stories] I. Title.
PZ7.0228Par   [Fic]   74-7479
ISBN 0-395-19495-4

COPYRIGHT (C) 1974 BY JANET O'DANIEL CICCHETTI
ALL RIGHTS RESERVED. NO PART OF THIS WORK MAY BE
REPRODUCED OR TRANSMITTED IN ANY FORM BY ANY MEANS,
ELECTRONIC OR MECHANICAL, INCLUDING PHOTOCOPYING AND
RECORDING, OR BY ANY INFORMATION STORAGE OR RETRIEVAL
SYSTEM, WITHOUT PERMISSION IN WRITING FROM THE PUBLISHER.
PRINTED IN THE UNITED STATES OF AMERICA
FIRST PRINTING C

A Part for
Addie

1

$\sim$

ADDIE TRIMBLE'S teeth were strong enough to crack
walnuts, and her father, Terence, always told her this would
assure her future in the theater. A leading lady could have
all the talent and beauty there was, but when her teeth
started to go she was finished. It was more a joke than
anything — Terence loved a good laugh — but there was
truth in it too. Lottie Millhaus, who had been taken on as
leading lady for the Bowen Theatrical Company for the
summer tour, was such a one with her pale skin, dark eyes
and misty brown hair. A regular beauty and no denying it.
But she already had a gap in her teeth. Far enough back so
it wasn't readily noticed, but still she had to watch out for
full smiles when facing an audience.

In the matter of teeth Addie took after Terence himself,
who was missing only one and that as a result of a fall from
General Strong, his grand trouping horse. A Philadelphia
dentist had replaced the missing member with a whalebone

1

peg, which was a masterpiece of dental art. And to Terence's credit, he had never blamed the General. They were alike in other ways too, Addie and her father — sandy-haired, skinny and supple — and both of them practical and sharp, near with a dollar although not what you would call tight-fisted. And both of them watched over Rose-Anne with gimlet-eyed protectiveness. Beauty like Rose-Anne's could be a heavy cross, as Terence had pointed out more than once.

The three of them were billed as The Dancing Trimbles. There had been four until last year when Addie's mother died. The three remaining had gone on, of course. It was what they did — their livelihood. It seemed to Addie that Terence had never been the same since her mother's death. There was a good deal more brandy consumed these days; it didn't seem to affect Terence's dancing in any way, but it was a thing Addie disliked and, being a disciplined person, disapproved of. She kept all this to herself. It would not have been fitting, she thought, to discuss it with Rose-Anne or indeed anyone else. It would have been stretching if not really breaking a Commandment. But responsibilities were mounting, piling and bunching up like thunderheads off in the distance. There were going to be rough times ahead, Addie sensed.

Tonight, however, she was concentrating on the business at hand, running over lines and cues in her head because she had a small part in *The Lover's Letter*, the play they were performing this week as part of the bill at the Pickens Public Inn (altered through long years of hasty pronunciation to the Pig and Pelican). Now she tied on her apron and reached up to see that her white ruffled cap was secure. She

2

took a note out of the apron pocket and climbed the three steps to the stage behind the scenery. Then she reached down and knocked smartly on the floor so that the audience seated out front in the tavern's public room could hear it clearly.

"Come in!"

Addie pushed open the painted door and entered.

"Yes? What is it?" The tone was imperious and the young woman who turned toward Addie looked proud and beautiful, with dark eyes against pale skin and dark hair falling around her shoulders. Dumb as a hitching post, Addie thought with some resignation, hoping Lottie would manage to remember her lines tonight.

"It's a note, Miss. The gentleman left it."

"A note — " Lottie took a step toward the small table with its single candle that stood stage center. Addie held the note extended and Lottie's eyes went to it, but she did not take it. She seemed suddenly paralyzed. Forgotten her lines, Addie thought savagely. She tried to furnish a cue.

"He said I should give it to you."

The paralysis changed to panic. Without warning, Lottie collapsed in a heavy faint, none too graceful.

Addie stared in disbelief, while thinking fast. Lottie was supposed to read the note aloud and then faint. But there she lay like a horse with the heaves and the plot still unexplained. Addie hastened to improvise. She hurried to Lottie and knelt beside her, unfolded the note and read it aloud in clear projecting tones.

" 'I knew when I left you this afternoon that all was lost. When you read this I will be in a better world.' Poor lady,"

3

Addie murmured sadly. "She must have *guessed* what was in it."

She held the kneeling pose, her head bowed in sorrow, while the curtain closed. The applause was quick and heartfelt and there were one or two audible sobs. Addie got up and then Lottie scrambled to her feet, hind end first like a cow. Addie held herself in check lest she aim a kick at Lottie's rear. Without looking back, Addie skipped down the three steps to the room behind the stage and began pulling off her cap and untying her apron. Lottie's voice followed her, whimpering and resentful.

"Well, Mr. Bowen changed my last line today, if you must know, and it mixed me up; that's all. No call for you to act so big about it."

Addie, refusing to listen, began to whistle loudly as she ducked behind the sheet strung up to form a dressing room. Maybelle Sweeney, the soprano, was waiting there to help her, her plump face red with suppressed laughter.

"Oh, Lord, that was fine, Addie," she chuckled. "You should've seen her royal highness turn purple when she realized Lottie'd blown up in her lines."

They both peeked over the sheet, watching as Mrs. Millhaus shepherded her daughter out.

"Lovely, dear!" Mrs. Millhaus was exclaiming with enough volume for all to hear. "Charming bit of improvisation!"

Maybelle Sweeney shook her head.

"Poor Lottie's going to catch it as soon as Mama gets her in their room."

Addie peeled out of the maid's costume, down to her vest and drawers, and slipped into the sailor outfit that she wore

4

for the closing number on the bill — white trousers, middy blouse, short blue jacket, ribboned hat. She wore soft black dancing shoes and carried a baton.

"Where's Papa and Rose-Anne?"

"Just coming in."

Addie glanced over the sheet again. Terence and Rose-Anne were entering, dressed in costumes that matched hers. That door connected with the tavern's backstairs and the private rooms on the second floor. Why were they coming in that way? Had Rose-Anne had to go looking for him? Had Terence gone up to his room after their opening number? And if so, had he gone there for brandy?

She waved her baton at them to indicate she was ready. Maybelle finished braiding her hair for her and tied the plait with a red ribbon.

"There you go, dearie."

"Thank you, Maybelle."

From the other side of the raised stage with its closed curtain came the sound of a hornpipe as the musicians struck up the closing number. Thaddeus Bowen, the manager, perspiring in the heat of the summer night, motioned to them agitatedly.

"You're on, Trimbles!"

He was a short, paunchy man who always did perspire a great deal, even in winter. He knew his business and was not, as Terence remarked, a bad fellow to work for, but Addie had never found him personally likable. He wore full side whiskers and a trimmed beard. Sometimes on these summer tours he filled in at small parts — kindly judges, wise doctors — but he never gave himself many lines, for he disliked memorizing.

5

Terence Trimble winked at Addie and flicked his baton nonchalantly, not hurrying despite the manager's prodding. He crossed the cluttered room with graceful strides and mounted the three steps to the stage, slipping behind the painted flats and out of sight. A sound of applause came as the curtain opened. Addie and Rose-Anne stood by the steps waiting for their cue. Terence always did a short solo turn around the stage before bringing them on.

"Is Papa all right?" Addie whispered.

Rose-Anne nodded without speaking and Addie glanced at her. She seemed calm enough — a little pale perhaps. The two of them stood without saying anything, waiting for their cue. When it came — a long flutter on the drum — they skipped up the three steps without even glancing at each other for confirmation. They had done it times without number. On the small lamplit stage they went at once into the figures of the hornpipe, giving only brief bows to acknowledge the applause. They twirled, pointed their toes in the black slippers, circled around Terence, danced back to back with their batons held over their heads. The music's tempo picked up and they danced faster. This finale always brought the audience around to footstamping and handclapping. Bowen had given the Trimbles the closing spot only two weeks ago after he had seen what a hit they were with audiences all along the tour. Lottie Millhaus and her mother had been very cross about it because it was the choicest spot on the bill. But Bowen who, Addie suspected, was sweet on Lottie or maybe on her mother — she was not sure which — was first a businessman, and audiences liked the Trimbles. They liked the pounding music, the tricky footwork, and they liked the picture the three of them made. Terence stood as slim and supple as a boy with his sandy hair and bright blue eyes, and he danced as gracefully as he had at eighteen. On one side of him was Rose-Anne, all pink and honey gold, smiling at the audience, and on the other side Addie, an inch taller than her sister and a little more angular, but just as light on her feet.

The two girls circled Terence, then pulled away while he did a fast and intricate step that was partly a jig, wobbly legged and fast. Then the three of them locked arms, batons held crosswise in front of them, and went into their big closing. The audience jumped up and started cheering. Bowen himself worked the curtain closed, but opened it again as the applause thundered on. The Dancing Trimbles did one more quick turn around the stage and Bowen closed the curtain again.

Terence seemed pleased as the three of them went backstage down the three steps.

"Very nice, girls," he said. "A very good week."

Addie glanced up at him. They were all flushed and panting, but Terence's look was a satisfied one, and she thought he had been pleased by the audience. She hurried in to seize what looked like a good opportunity.

"Well, why don't we celebrate, then, Papa? I'll get a tray of supper from Mrs. Pickens and we'll have it upstairs — a little party, like old times."

The minute she mentioned old times she knew she had put it wrong. Distress passed over Terence's face like one of Bowen's scrim curtains.

"Fine idea," Terence said lightly. "But you girls go ahead. I'll be along after a bit. I want to talk to Billy about something."

7

He gave them each a pat and then walked away across the room, through the confusion of musicians, scenery, piles of costumes. Addie glanced at Rose-Anne and saw that her eyes were following Terence bleakly. Addie felt she ought to voice some kind of reassurance, yet deception was not a thing she cared for. Besides, Rose-Anne was fifteen — pretty grown up. She would know the truth whether Addie tried to smooth it over or not.

"He'll be all right," Addie said at last. "Billy'll keep an eye on him." And they watched together as Terence went over and joined Billy Buncombe, the comic, against the opposite wall. Billy was still wearing his short wide trousers, his too-tight jacket and his too-small hat. He had done his Foxy Feathers monologue tonight, about a fox in a henhouse. It was always well received by country audiences. He was Maybelle Sweeney's husband, but each had separate billing; usually it was "The Incomparable Mrs. Sweeney and the Risible Mr. Buncombe." The Trimbles were closer to Billy and Maybelle than to anyone else in the company. During the regular theater season they shared the same boarding house just off Chestnut Street in Philadelphia. If Terence started drinking tonight, Addie was sure Billy could be counted on to see that he behaved himself and to get him upstairs.

"I'm tired," Addie said presently. "Let's go on up to bed." She was not tired at all, but keyed up, excited as she always was after a good performance. It would be hours before she felt like sleeping. But Rose-Anne looked played out and Addie worried about her. "You go ahead, Rose-Anne. I'll go out to the kitchen and ask Mrs. Pickens for bread and milk to bring up."

8

Rose-Anne nodded and left and Addie watched her go, her walk dispirited but her back still straight and somehow elegant. All the Trimbles knew how to carry themselves.

She carried up a more festive tray than she had planned on, for Mrs. Pickens pressed upon her two chicken breasts roasted with a sprinkle of nutmeg, and a bowl of new raspberries. A late supper far too rich for dancers, and Addie knew it, but something in the temper of the night called for reassurance — even a touch of celebration. Rose-Anne was quick to catch the mood and they ate until they were wickedly stuffed and had laughed over and over about Lottie Millhaus and her gaffes. It was late by the time they had undressed and knelt by the bed to say their prayers.

Once in bed Rose-Anne slept immediately and soundly, but Addie had a harder time falling asleep. Thoughts were flaring around in her head, gibbering and mocking and keeping her awake. Thoughts about Terence, thoughts about their future. The more she tried to let go and relax, the thicker and faster they came. And through it all she kept listening for the sound of Terence's footsteps in the hall outside. When she heard them at last, Billy's were with them and that relieved her. She sized up the manner of their walking. Steady enough, she thought. Their voices were elaborately hushed, much louder than Terence and Billy thought them. She heard their two doors close, one after the other. Then the inn was silent except for a few sounds from far away downstairs. Slamming of shutters and a few clanking noises. That would be Mr. Pickens closing up, making things fast for the night. Worry, which had been picking at Addie all evening with sharp fingers, at last let go. She felt herself going limp and sinking down into warm darkness.

A rumbling sound like faraway thunder woke her sometime later. She raised herself on one elbow and looked around. There was no sign of dawn at the window yet. Was a storm coming? The men hereabouts had been haying all week. She supposed a thunderstorm would spoil it for them. It would make the roads muddy too, for traveling, she thought sleepily. She sank back on the pillow, luxuriously snug, and waited for the storm to come nearer. Then in an instant of sudden knowledge Addie's eyes flew open to the darkness and to a room that seemed, in the summer night, frighteningly cold. It was no sound of thunder she had heard. Something had happened. The sound was inside the inn.

A door opened and closed and there were footsteps in the hall. She glanced at Rose-Anne, who still slept, then lifted the covers and swung her feet over the side of the bed. Barefooted and breathing shallowly she went to the door and opened it. The hall was dark and Addie had no candle, but she could make out a stout shape coming toward her — Maybelle in her tentlike nightdress.

"Never mind, dear, just go back," Maybelle said urgently. Her soft flesh enveloped Addie, and Addie could hear her rapid breathing.

"No!" Addie shouted, suddenly frightened. "What's going on?" And she pushed past Maybelle down the dark corridor toward the stairs where a faint light glowed. When she reached them she put both hands out, touching the wall on either side, and looked down. It was a steep narrow flight of stairs, dark and shadowy. At the bottom of it someone stood holding a candle high.

"Papa?" Addie said sharply. "Billy?"

The hand that held the candle trembled and the light wavered. Billy turned and looked up at her. His plain comic's face was white; his mouth trembled loosely. And now Addie saw that something lay at his feet — a heap or bundle or pile.

"Addie darlin', go back with Maybelle. You mustn't — I heard something — I couldn't tell what it was — and I came out — " Hot tallow was dripping onto the front of Billy's nightshirt, but he seemed not to feel it. "It's your papa, Addie. He seems to have fallen."

2

THEY BURIED Terence Trimble on Monday afternoon in a small burying ground that lay along the main road west from Albany. Addie could not help thinking how far it was from the Chestnut Street theater in Philadelphia, how far from the city crowds and the muddy city streets that had been familiar to him in life. Still, it was a decent burial and the young preacher who spoke the words did so with suitable respect, she thought. The grave was in a pleasant spot near a spreading copper beech.

"It's pretty bare, isn't it, Addie?" Rose-Anne whispered, nodding toward the new grave and the plain wooden marker.

"We'll take care of that," Addie reassured her, glancing at Rose-Anne as she had a hundred times the past two days to see if she was all right. But Rose-Anne, whose soft golden beauty always looked as if it would bruise like a fallen peach, had a backbone of iron. She had let out a long moan when Addie told her what had happened, and she had turned white, but after that she had not given way. Even when they talked about Terence, she kept hold of herself.

"He was awful unhappy, wasn't he, Addie?"

"I guess he was, yes."

"Well, now he's in heaven with Mama."

"Yes." Addie hadn't gone so far as to seize on the comfort of the heaven idea yet, but the part about his being unhappy was certainly true. It was the one thing that kept haunting her now. What torments had he been going through there in the lonely night? What agonies had kept him awake and restless so that at last he had gone careening out in the dark, down the treacherous steep stairs in search of more brandy? Addie had not discussed that part of it with Rose-Anne, but she knew well enough that was what had happened.

The whole company was at the service, from Thaddeus Bowen right on through the whole cast, the scenery men and musicians. Maybelle was puffy and red from weeping. Billy Buncombe's homely face was sober and twitching. Even the two Millhauses came, Lottie and her mother, and both looked genuinely shocked. The innkeeper and his wife were there and the stout Mrs. Pickens kept shaking her head and whispering softly, "Such a handsome fellow."

Addie listened sharply to the young clergyman, a shade apprehensive that he might go into the sin and frivolity aspect of theater life and the grim need for repentence. But to her surprise he quoted 2 Samuel and reminded them all gently that David had danced to the glory of the Lord. Addie considered it a thoughtful remark. Then the coffin was lowered into the ground by Bowen, Billy Buncombe,

13

Tom Every, who was the leading man, and Abner Merritt, the violin player and a friend of Terence's for many years.

With amazing ease, then, it was over, and they all returned to the Pig and Pelican. One by one everyone asked Addie and Rose-Anne if there was anything he could do to help and the two girls said no thank you, they were fine. Then they shook hands all around and climbed the stairs to their room. They took off their bonnets and sat down, Rose-Anne on the edge of the bed and Addie in the chair by the window. It was a sunny day and the smell of cut hay was coming in through the open window from the fields beyond the inn, where men were working with their scythes. A fly buzzed in and careened around the room, loud in the stillness.

Rose-Anne looked at Addie with wide blue eyes.

"It all really happened, didn't it?"

Addie nodded, preparing herself for what was coming, because of course it would come.

"I was just thinking, sitting here," Rose-Anne went on, "about how there used to be four of us — you know, Mama and Papa and the two of us. And then when Mama died we thought it was the end of everything and Papa — well, I don't think he was ever the same, but we went on. And now there's just us."

"Yes," Addie said, waiting.

Rose-Anne sat perfectly still for a few minutes and then her eyes slowly filled with tears and the corners of her mouth twitched and she started to sob. And presently she leaned over sideways on the bed and buried her face in the pillow and kept on sobbing. Addie waited for a minute and then went over to the bed and hoisted Rose-Anne's feet up on it. She sat down beside her, perched on the edge, and patted Rose-Anne's back for a long time. The sobs became more widely spaced and the snuffling deeper. Addie pulled a light cover over her sister and went back to the chair by the window. It would do Rose-Anne good to sleep for a time.

Well, now it was her turn, she thought to herself. If she wanted to let go, now was the moment, with Rose-Anne asleep and no one to see. And, indeed, she could feel the tears behind her eyes, the fullness in her throat. Of course, she answered herself sensibly, once you let go it will be easier to do it next time. If you give in to it, it might get to be a habit. There's a lot of planning and figuring to be done pretty quickly here and somebody has to stay sharp and do it.

She straightened her back and stared through narrowed eyes out of the window at the distant hay cutters. At last she moved a trifle and raised one hand to the gold brooch at the collar of her dark gray dress. It had been her mother's brooch and touching it seemed a reassurance. She got up and glanced at Rose-Anne, who slept more peacefully now. Addie tiptoed out of the room.

She found Bowen in the public room downstairs, sitting at a table with Tom Every, the leading man, a pleasant-faced and capable young man of no outstanding talent, but reliable and a quick study. The public room was quiet, for it was a working day and still early. Both men got up when they saw her.

"You all right, Addie?" Tom asked quickly. She had known him since he was playing page parts and singing boy soprano.

15

"I'm fine, Tom," she replied. "Just wanted to see Mr. Bowen for a minute."

"I'll leave you, then."

Tom strolled outside with his hands in his pockets and Addie sat down at the table opposite Bowen. She felt oddly formal, wearing her Sunday dress on a weekday afternoon. Across from her the manager looked sympathetic.

"Well, my dear, how is your sister bearing up?" he asked, and Addie knew it was an attempt at being kind. Still, it did not escape her that he assumed *she* would be bearing up all right.

"Why, not too bad, Mr. Bowen. She's resting right now."

"Ah, very beneficial. Knitting up 'the ravel'd sleave of care,' as the Bard put it so well."

"Yes." Addie hesitated for a moment. Then, "Mr. Bowen," she went on, plunging into it. "I realize you'll be going ahead with tonight's performance."

Bowen looked troubled and touched his side whiskers.

"Well, now. I surely do hate to have to do that, Addie. I just can't tell you how I hate it. But the thing of it is, the handbills are out, all around these parts. When we decided to stay another week — Saturday it was — I sent Paddy around with 'em, and of course people will be coming."

"Yes, I know that. That was what I wanted to talk to you about." Addie paused, feeling her heart start to pound. She hurried on with it. "My sister and I will be appearing as usual, Mr. Bowen. I wanted you to know so you could plan the bill. I thought you might feel backward about asking us to, but it's all right. It's exactly what Papa would have wanted us to do."

16

"Why, Addie, indeed I never would have asked — "

"No, it's all right," she insisted. "And what about the play? Will we be doing *Lover's Letter* again?"

"Why, no, I thought we'd change to *Fortune's Folly* tonight. But we could leave out your part — "

Addie shook her head. Her part was a young country girl, not many lines, and she knew it well.

"No, I'll do it," she said. "Now as far as the handbills go, I think we can just leave them, don't you? We're billed as the Dancing Trimbles and the name still fits."

"You're going on with the tour then? You're staying with the company?"

"Oh, certainly," Addie replied at once.

"I only wondered. I thought you might have some family — relatives. Two young ladies alone — "

"We don't consider it alone, sir. We have Billy and Maybelle. And yourself, of course," she added politely.

"What about the act?" Bowen asked. "It'll need work—"

"I've given it some thought. I'll work the music changes out with Abner and if you like I can explain to you what I plan to do." She saw him hesitate and knew what was on his mind. "About our salary," she said.

"Well. Now as to that — " His eyes grew narrow and cagey.

"Thirty-five dollars a week was what the three of us got. Of course Rose-Anne and I would expect to get something less."

"I'd say about fifteen would be fair," Bowen suggested with the expansive air of someone making a generous gesture.

17

"Twenty-five was about what I thought."

"For two young ladies of limited experience, I don't know —"

"Of course I'd still do the opening number on the slack wire."

He was silent and she could tell he was considering it, weighing the value of the act. She knew it was a good one; audiences liked it. Terence had come on first, walking the wire in his easy light way, and then Addie would follow him and she would make it look hard, pretending to lose her balance, almost falling, regaining her footing, with Terence looking at her in terror all the time.

"Rose-Anne wouldn't be on the wire," he pointed out. "There'd be just you."

"Yes, but she can be onstage with me to do the effects. And I'm working with her all the time. In a few weeks she'll be ready for the wire too."

"Well, with the wire act, perhaps eighteen dollars."

"Suppose we say twenty-two — until Rose-Anne's ready."

"I don't think you'd find any theater manager in Philadelphia prepared to pay that kind of salary to —"

She cut him off. "Of course without the wire act you won't have any real spectacle. And for us to stay on just for the dance number at fifteen dollars, I really don't think we'd be interested."

She watched him thinking that over, keeping her expression calm and even rather offhand, but inside feeling nervous and hoping she had not shown too much brass. If he decided to let them go, what would become of them?

18

She watched as he got up from the table and crossed the room, hands thrust into his pockets. His head was down, doubling his chin, and he scowled at the floor.

"I might consider twenty," he said, walking back. He looked unhappy about it.

Then he wants us, Addie thought.

"I believe my figure of twenty-two is fair," she said carefully. "And twenty-five when Rose-Anne goes on the wire. But for that I would be willing to throw in our horse Blossom. We will keep General Strong, of course." She knew for a fact that Bowen could use another horse, for one of his had pulled up lame, and transporting scenery and props was always a problem.

Bowen looked harried, weighing gain against loss, making hasty calculations in his head. At last he lifted one hand in a gesture of giving in. Now what can I do? the hand seemed to say. I'm not a hard man.

"Well, that's that, then," Addie said in a businesslike way. She got up and extended her hand which Bowen took in a damp grasp. "And if that concludes our discussion of business I'll go back up to Rose-Anne. We'll be ready as usual tonight."

There was a rustling sound and then footsteps and Mrs. Millhaus swept down the stairs and into the room, handsome in stiff black silk. Her eyes darted from Bowen to Addie.

"Ah, Mr. Bowen," she said in her loud firm voice, "I wanted to discuss the evening's bill with you. There will be changes, of course. Adelina, my dear, you should be resting."

"Thank you, Mrs. Millhaus," Addie said primly. "It's kind of you to suggest it. But I've just told Mr. Bowen my sister and I will appear as usual."

For a naked second Mrs. Millhaus's face worked with annoyance as she realized that she had arrived on the scene too late. Then at once she recovered herself.

"Ah, well, very courageous of you I'm sure."

"Now perhaps I will rest for a while," Addie said, dropping a quick curtsy and making her exit. Behind her Mrs. Millhaus was saying, "*Fortune's Folly* tonight? Splendid. Lottie and I have only now been going over our parts — "

Addie worried about Rose-Anne in spite of the show of confidence she had put up in front of Bowen. When she returned to their room she refrained from waking her, letting her sleep on through the long summer afternoon. At last Maybelle knocked timidly and entered with a tray containing a pitcher of milk and some corn bread. Addie told her what she was planning. Maybelle's eyes went to Rose-Anne on the bed.

"Will she be all right, do you think?"

"I'm sure she will," Addie replied, not sure at all. "If we don't appear, Mrs. Millhaus will manage to get us out of the company in no time. I just know it."

"I wouldn't put it past Bowen."

"And we need the work, Maybelle. How would we live?"

Maybelle looked uncertain. Then she said, still in low tones, "Addie, I've been thinking about all this and talking with Billy about it. He said I should speak to you, but I thought to wait a day or two. It isn't as if you don't have family, you know. Your mother came from this part of the country somewhere. Those people, whoever they are, they're your kin."

"They'd be just strangers to us, Maybelle."

"Well, and so they would. But people don't stay strangers forever. Billy said that on Saturday, that last night, when he and your papa were talking downstairs, you know? He said that your papa spoke of it — of your grandpa's place — and whether you and Rose-Anne mightn't be better off going there to stay for a time."

"Papa said that?" Addie was astounded.

"He did, Addie, that's the truth. Maybe he knew — I mean, maybe something told him — you know — what was coming. Oh, dear, I didn't mean to talk about it today, but it's something you should think about."

Addie kissed her suddenly on the cheek.

"What would we ever do without you, Maybelle? Now don't stew about us. I've talked to Bowen and it's all arranged. We're going to be fine. Time enough to worry in the fall when we get back to Philadelphia."

Maybelle brightened a little.

"Yes, goodness, time enough to worry then. All right, darlin', you just bang on my door if you need me."

After Maybelle had gone, Addie took the tray over to the stand beside the bed. She sat down by Rose-Anne, feeling a sudden anxiety, a heavy fear in her stomach. What if Rose-Anne flew all to pieces? What if she couldn't go on? She sat there for a few minutes. From next door she could hear the sound of Maybelle's clear sweet soprano running up and down scales. Addie put out a hand and touched her sister's shoulder. Rose-Anne was lying on her side with her back to Addie. At the touch of Addie's hand she rolled over on her back and turned her face toward Addie, eyes wide and staring. Addie spoke quickly.

"Time to wake up, Rose-Anne. Maybelle brought us a tray. Let's have something to eat, and then we'll sit and talk a little. We must decide a few things before the performance tonight. You'll have to give me some help in the wire act and we'll do the hornpipe differently." She said it quickly, not building up to it at all.

For a few moments Rose-Anne just stared at her with wide eyes and Addie could not tell whether she was still dazed by sleep or whether she was going to cry out and start sobbing again. Then Rose-Anne pushed herself up to a half-sitting position and raised a hand to push back her hair. It was damp and disheveled. For a few seconds she seemed to be getting herself together. And then she said, "All right, now, I'm awake. You just tell me what you want me to do, Addie."

Addie looked at her sister and swallowed, finding it a good deal harder this time to keep from crying.

3

THE PERFORMANCE went without a hitch. With almost no rehearsal Rose-Anne went through all the pantomime of the slack wire act, feigning horror when Addie teetered wildly, applauding with delight when Addie made it across the wire, even adding a clever little touch of her own, leaning over to draw an imaginary chalk line on the stage and pretending to walk it herself. The audience called them back twice. And when they closed the evening with the hornpipe, Rose-Anne was as buoyant and smiling as she had ever been. When they left the stage Addie almost told her how splendid she'd been, but she held back, feeling in some strong instinctive way that it would diminish Rose-Anne's self-respect. Rose-Anne had done exactly what Terence had taught them to do — carry on no matter what — and to make any great fuss about it would make it look as if no one had expected her to be up to it. Addie was even a little surprised when Abner Merritt, loosening his bowstrings and putting his violin away backstage, said to her, "You did real well, Addie. Terence would've been awful proud of you going on tonight."

Addie discovered that she had been so worried about Rose-Anne that she had never given much thought to whether she herself was up to it. She was touched and thanked Abner.

Next morning she worked with Rose-Anne on the slack wire for an hour, pleased with her progress and certain that she would be ready for the act in a short time. Then she put on her dark gray dress, brooch and bonnet once more and walked by herself a mile eastward along the road to a squared-log house that Mr. Pickens had described to her.

A small bent man in a heavy towcloth apron greeted her civilly and they stood in the sunny dooryard discussing business. When they had agreed on a price Addie took a slip of paper out of her pocket.

"These are the words I want on the stone," she said. She had sat up late the night before composing them. " 'These nimble feet shall dance no more, Save for the Lord at Heaven's door,' " she read aloud. "And then his name and dates, you see. I have it all written down. Is it clear enough?"

The man scanned the paper.

"Oh, it do be clear enough, Miss," he said politely. "But it don't seem entirely regular, mentioning dancing and the Lord, together that way. I mean — they's a good many verses you could pick from if you'd want me to say some of 'em over for ye. 'From sin and error now set free, He rests with angels heavenly.' That's a real nice one."

Out of courtesy Addie refrained from saying that she thought it about the worst bit of rhyming she had ever heard.

"No, this is exactly what I want," she said with firmness. "David danced to the glory of God, you know." And then she added severely, "Second Samuel."

Mention of the Scripture did seem to have an effect and he made no more argument. He went over the words and figures with her to be sure he had them exactly right and then she handed him two coins.

"I will be back this way later in the summer and will pay the balance when the stone is finished," she said. He nodded and bobbed his head and said he would get on with it right away.

Members of the troupe were having their noon meal around a big table at the inn when she returned. Rose-Anne was sitting at one end of the table next to Bowen, who seemed solicitous about passing her food and chatting with her. Addie slid into a place at the other end between Tom Every and Billy Buncombe, murmuring her excuses. She was glad to see that Rose-Anne had joined the others; relieved too that the usually indifferent Bowen was putting himself out a little to act pleasant.

Addie was beginning, for the first time in three days, to feel a loosening, an unwinding within herself. Nerves and muscles that had felt stretched and taut at last eased. Anxieties slid away from her. From across the table Maybelle winked and passed her a plate of ham, pink and juicy and falling in thin curled slices. Mrs. Millhaus, at Bowen's other hand, was saying in her clear stagy voice, "When my late husband was in the London theater — "

and "That was Charles Kemble in *Point of Honor*, wasn't it, Lottie? An excellent vehicle, I always thought — " But it did not bother Addie today — even the woman's heavy-handed domination of talk at the table. Today they were her family, close and dear, full of faults and vanities but hanging together in the small and special world of the theater where outsiders were never truly at home. It had been Terence's world, and now it was theirs — hers and Rose-Anne's — because they had earned a place in it. What they did they did as well as anybody, better than most. She felt so full of this knowledge, so brimming with the comfort of it, that she glanced down the table toward her sister to see if Rose-Anne was sharing any of it.

Rose-Anne sat still and pale next to Bowen. Her food was untouched on her plate. She lifted her water glass and the hand that held it trembled slightly. Finally her blue eyes caught Addie's over the rim of the glass, and it seemed to Addie they had a hollow, haunted look. Addie felt a sudden alarm. Had Rose-Anne come apart, then, after doing so well? Had Addie pushed too hard? She ate the rest of her dinner carelessly, not tasting the food, and when the others began to get up she hurried to Rose-Anne. But Rose-Anne was already up and moving toward the stairs.

"What is it? Is something wrong?" Addie demanded. "You look — "

Rose-Anne shook her head. "I'm going up to rest," she said.

"Are you sick?"

"Talk to Bowen," Rose-Anne said woodenly, and she moved away from Addie and fled up the stairs.

Addie turned back toward the table where Bowen sat,

26

sucking at his teeth and exchanging a few words with Abner Merritt and Billy, who were still at their places. Addie walked over to him.

"Mr. Bowen, my sister seems upset," she said abruptly.

Bowen rose politely, removing his napkin from his waistcoat.

"A rather becoming display of emotion. No cause for alarm, Addie."

Addie glanced at Billy and Abner, who were in conversation across the table.

"May we talk privately, Mr. Bowen? Perhaps on the veranda — "

She led the way and he followed. Addie could feel the coldness that had crept into her hands and feet and she did her best to control her breathing so that her words would come out normally.

"I just can't imagine what has happened," she began, turning to face him. "Rose-Anne was doing quite well."

Bowen, still looking pleased over his recent meal, lifted one hand in a small gesture of reassurance.

"A momentary reaction, my dear, nothing more. And as I say, becoming. I have just asked Rose-Anne to marry me."

"Marry you!"

"Yes, just this morning. Oh, I realize it's sudden, but all done with good reason. After our talk yesterday — "

"Marry Rose-Anne!"

" — it occurred to me that I have a great deal to offer in the way of security, protection, not to mention — ah — devotion."

He's older than Papa, Addie thought desperately.

"Rose-Anne's fifteen!"

27

"Young, but not too young. Many girls — "

He went on talking, but Addie heard only scraps of it. Her own thoughts went spinning. Just imagine! She had always thought he was sweet on Lottie or even Mrs. Millhaus. But all the time he must have been watching Rose-Anne, waiting for his chance.

"Then when I realized you'd both be staying on with the troupe, I thought, why not offer these two young ladies my protection — oh, you will share in that, Addie, I assure you — and when we return to Philadelphia you will automatically be members of the permanent company during the winter season. A great deal of prestige there, and I have no doubt Rose-Anne can soon take leading parts — with some coaching from me. A name like Mrs. Thaddeus Bowen would take her far, I can promise you."

"No." Addie dropped it like a stone.

"Now, no hasty decisions, please. I realize the idea is new to you — "

"No!"

"Well, now." Bowen was reddening and his side whiskers seemed to stand out angrily. "I felt I was doing the proper thing, speaking to you as her only relative."

Addie drew herself up primly.

"I am not Rose-Anne's only relative. Our grandfather, Mr. Jeremiah Drummond of — these parts — would gladly offer us a home."

"Are you sure?" Bowen looked wily. "Ever seen him?"

"Our father often mentioned — "

"Oh, sure. Might mean something if he was sober when he mentioned it." Bowen's voice had become a sneer. "On the other hand, how do you know your grandfather's alive still? And if he is, how do you know he'd want two draggletail heel-and-toe nobodies on his hands?"

"That's only one possibility," Addie replied icily.

"Well, if the other possibility's the theater, you can forget about that. You may think you've got a great act out here in the country, but back in Philadelphia there's a dozen better than you. And who do you know in the theater? Nobody but me."

Addie felt anger springing up from so many sources that she hardly knew how to stem it. With scarcely a pause to draw breath, Bowen had slandered Terence's memory, spoken slightingly of their grandfather and insulted them as performers. And all that on top of having the almighty sand to ask Rose-Anne to marry him!

"My sister and I will be leaving your employ and this place in the morning," she said in loud clear tones. "I consider it most unsuitable of you to bring up the subject of marriage when we are still mourning our father. It indicates to me that you are a man of no character whatever." She turned to go, paused in the doorway and turned back. "Our horse Blossom will not be at your disposal either."

29

4

THE GIRLS had walked the three miles from the village and the day was hot. Rose-Anne complained, but mildly; she was not a grumbler by nature.

"I don't think the General would have minded three more miles."

"He's carried us a long way," Addie said. "It isn't fair." It had bothered her to see the horse's head sinking lower, his feet plodding along the dusty road. "General Strong is a performer. We can't treat him like any old cart horse."

"What will they think when they see us, though? Look at our shoes!"

Addie looked down and saw that her shoes, like Rose-Anne's, were caked with dust.

"They'll think we're travelers come a long way — which we are. Besides, maybe it won't be *they*. Maybe it'll be just our grandfather."

"Living all alone?"

"Well — maybe. We know our grandmother's dead; Mama told us that. Remember?"

Rose-Anne unwrapped a small bundle.

"We'd better finish this johnnycake before we get there. We may not get to eat again for a while."

"They're not going to starve us."

"Still — "

There seemed to be some merit in the suggestion. They finished the johnnycake, then made their way, leading the General, down to a small clear stream near the road. The three of them drank and the girls washed their hands and faces and brushed at their shoes with leaves.

"There, now," Addie said. "We don't look any worse than two ladies just getting off the through stage from Albany."

"Addie — "

Addie glanced sharply at her sister, hearing the trembling note.

"Addie, suppose they don't want us?"

"Oh, what nonsense!" Addie heard her own voice — too loud, too strident. "It doesn't matter whether they want us or not. They have to do something for us. Besides, would you rather be back there with — you know — "

Rose-Anne shivered and looked cold in spite of the hot July day.

"No," she said weakly, and Addie felt like a bully. It was not Rose-Anne's fault, what had happened.

"Well, then," she said in a brighter tone. "Let's keep going. It must be just up ahead. Bear left where the road forks — we did that already — then watch for it on a rise to the right. Three miles, they said, and I'm sure we've walked

31

that far or near to it." She tugged at General Strong's bridle and they climbed back up to the road. Their shoes were coated again before they had gone a half-dozen steps.

It was certainly mortal strange, Addie reflected as they walked, how they had undertaken this journey, but she could not see, no matter how she turned the matter this way and that to look at it, how they could have done anything else. They were certainly going into the unknown and it was only by chance that they had even known in which direction to head after her fine defiant exit lines to Bowen. Only by chance and a first-rate actor's memory which had enabled Billy Buncombe to come up with the name of the village he had heard Terence mention in connection with their grandfather. "The village of Barker Mills, or near to it — " which was all they had to go on. Yet Barker Mills existed. It was a real place and real places could be located. Mr. Pickens, the innkeeper, had provided the first help. "Why, that's to westward, and it might be just a shade north. Take the main road as far as Parson's Ford and then head northerly. Ask along the way."

"We'll find it," Addie had said confidently, setting her chin at a slight tilt that recalled Terence.

"Oh, to be sure you will," Maybelle had quavered, trying to keep her voice steady. "And your grandpa will be ever so glad to see you, I just know." At which she had burst into a freshet of weeping which necessitated their all crowding around to comfort her, and only after that was accomplished had they been able to settle down to arrangements.

"We can't take both Blossom and the General," Addie said practically, "so it's got to be the General."

"Blossom's good and steady," Billy pointed out.

32

"Yes, but General Strong was Papa's horse," Addie said, and no one offered any more argument. "Only I want Blossom in good hands. What do you think?"

"Try Pickens," Billy suggested, and this had proved to be the solution. Mr. Pickens, a little choked up himself, had taken both Blossom and the rig and had paid them a more handsome price than Addie thought reasonable, but he had insisted, pressing the coins into her hand damply and saying over and over, "Now you little ladies stop back this way, you hear?" Addie assured him that they would, since there was still the matter of Terence's stone to be concluded.

And so it was on the General that they had left early the next morning, with Billy and Maybelle up to see them off, and with a spate of encouragement, caveats, promises and expectations falling around their heads. "We'll see you in Philadelphia in the autumn — By then we'll be able to get shut of Bowen ourselves and make new plans — Maybe we'll even try New York City — Now don't stop anyplace that looks even a shade rough, darlings — a farmhouse generally is a safe bet — If it's a town, look for a place where ladies go — "

And then the dust of the road and silence and Maybelle and Billy small figures far behind.

As it turned out, they had no trouble finding directions to Barker Mills. Farmers and tradesmen along the way were helpful. When they reached the village itself after three days' travel and asked directions to their grandfather's house they were surprised at the note of deference they encountered. Mr. Jeremiah Drummond was spoken of in tones of respect which caused Addie a small feeling of pride. It did not entirely crowd out the other feeling that lay there crouched and cold, but that was something Addie was determined not to pay any mind to. When you had no one else to turn to, you turned to kin; that was all there was to it.

"Addie, look!" Rose-Anne's voice was high with excitement. "Do you suppose that's it? It must be!"

The house stood back from the road on a slight rise — a big house of rose brick with white trim. A huge oak tree stood in front of it, reaching its branches over to touch the gray slate roof. Stone steps led up to the white front door. Ivy grew up one side wall, softening the corner of the house.

Addie and Rose-Anne stood still in the road and studied it for a moment. Behind them General Strong moved his head impatiently and shook away flies. A long gentle slope of green led up to the house. Some distance behind it there were barns and outbuildings. The little town of Barker Mills which they had just passed through had been only a few log and frame houses, a smithy and a church, but this house, standing by itself, looked unbelievably fine — the kind of house, Addie thought, where your knock would be answered by an apple-cheeked servant girl in a white apron.

"Our grandfather must be — quite well off," Rose-Anne said tactfully.

Addie nodded. The discovery was a surprise, yet she found that it made little difference to her. She had no plan to make their grandfather's house any permanent haven. This was a makeshift, something to tide them over until they could find their way back to Philadelphia or perhaps New York and to the stage. Addie was at heart no country girl and affluence in the country did not look the same to her as affluence in the city. She saw no particular advantage in it

34

even, for what could anyone do with money here? No shops, no carriages, no theaters. Still, there was one great advantage to the discovery. It was obvious that in asking for some small temporary assistance they would not be creating a hardship for their grandfather, and this was a relief.

"Well, let's go," she said, tugging at the General's bridle.

And so they walked, one on each side of the big white horse, up the hard-packed lane that led to the front door. Glancing sideways at Rose-Anne, Addie could see excitement in her sister's face. Rose-Anne's cheeks were flushed with color and she put up a hand now and then to adjust her bonnet. Addie felt, rather than excitement, a kind of dull regret that their three days of travel were over. It had been a wonderful free time, like a holiday, traveling from village to village and farm to farm. She was almost sad that it was done, because it was the kind of adventure that might never come again. Once they had even slept out under the stars.

They tied General Strong to a stone hitching post at the foot of the front steps and climbed up. They glanced at each other, hesitating for only a moment. Then Addie raised her hand and knocked smartly.

No neat curtsying country girl answered. No one answered at all. Addie frowned and knocked again. For a time there was no sound from inside. Then, coming from a distance, as though far to the back of the house, a voice could be heard, shouting or exclaiming. It was followed by footsteps and the door was flung open suddenly. A young man stood there in a sweat-stained work shirt and homespun breeches. His heavy work boots were lumpy with dirt and there was a strong, unmistakable smell of barn about

35

him. He was eating something. He stared at them without a trace of friendliness.

"Yes? What is it?" He was still chewing.

"Is this the Drummond house?" Addie inquired coolly.

"Yes," he said, glancing at Rose-Anne.

"Is Mr. Jeremiah Drummond at home? We'd like to see him."

"What for?" he asked rudely.

Addie held on to her temper.

"We just want to see him. May we?"

"I don't know if you can or not. Who are you, anyway?"

Addie did not budge.

"Would you call Mr. Drummond, please?"

"Well, I can't do that, but wait a minute — I mean — you can come in if you want to." And he stepped aside to let them enter. Addie had an impression, countering her first one of deliberate rudeness, that the young man was, rather, distracted, not concentrating on them entirely. He seemed irritated, as if thinking about something else; their coming was apparently an interruption.

"Wait here a minute," he said, and went off toward the back of the house. There were pounding footsteps and Addie guessed at the existence of a back stairway.

The front entrance hall where they stood was dim, but they could see that it was spacious and that a stairway with a graceful railing came down its center. There were archways to right and left and a corridor running to the back. The two rooms through the archways seemed to be parlors.

The girls stood without speaking while they waited. They heard a distant door slam and then angry voices from far

36

away. After a time it was quiet again. They exchanged a look and inspected the house around them. Rose-Anne breathed softly, " 'Tisn't much like the outside, is it?"

Addie shook her head. The house was fine enough, but completely uncared-for — dusty, dim, untidy. Curtains hung askew, heavy draperies were pulled crookedly over windows, and one had a great rip in its hem. Dustballs danced on the front stairway and muddy footprints made a path toward the back of the house.

"Looks as if Grandfather could do with a good housekeeper," Rose-Anne whispered.

Addie nodded, but she was straining her ears to hear more from upstairs. Presently the footsteps clumped down again, but the abrupt young man did not appear. She guessed he had gone out into the kitchen at the back. For several minutes the girls waited in the hall. Then a light footstep sounded on the stairs directly above them and there was a rustling sound. They looked up. A handsome, dark-haired woman stood there, looking imperious in spite of the dustballs around her feet. She had come only halfway down the stairs and there she stood, hand on the railing, looking down at them.

"How do you do? I am Caroline Drummond," she said with dignity. "My son says you wish to see me."

Addie collected her thoughts quickly. She certainly had not said that. And who could Caroline Drummond be anyway? The way she stood there, feet firmly planted, back straight, hand grasping the railing, she must be somebody. Addie decided she had better get hold of the situation by a good strong handle and turn it around her way.

"How do you do, Mrs. Drummond?" she asked brightly.

"I'm sure our arrival must come as a surprise to you. Let me introduce myself. I am Adelina Trimble, and this is my sister, Rose-Anne." She spoke clearly, enunciating as she had learned to do for audiences. "We are granddaughters to Mr. Jeremiah Drummond and we are here to visit him. We would like to pay our respects to our grandfather and to bring him some family news. We may also venture to impose on his hospitality for a short time." She thought it sounded like a passably good opening speech.

The woman stared down at them and frowned.

"What?" she said rather stupidly. "What was all that?"

For a brief few seconds Addie studied her closely, then decided on a more direct approach.

"May we see our Grandfather Drummond? We've traveled some distance to visit him. We're the Trimble girls."

Caroline Drummond's eyes went from Addie to Rose-Anne, then back again; as Addie watched she could see the eyes lose focus and turn glassy.

"Trimble?" she repeated.

Addie studied the situation. She had had enough experience this past year to recognize a drunkard when she saw one, but the question was, what to do next? She moved a step closer to the stairway, knowing for a certainty that the woman's hand on the railing was all that was holding her upright; it seemed she might pitch forward any second. Rose-Anne moved with her and the glance she slanted at Addie indicated she had sized up the situation too. Addie harbored quick resentful thoughts against the muddy young man who had left them in this kind of fix.

They were saved from the moment of decision by the

opening of the door behind them. Two men came in out of the bright sunlight, their footsteps loud and careless in the dusty hall.

"Ah! Here they are — just arrived." The older of the two men, tall and with graying hair, smiled warmly at them. He glanced up the stairway at the woman, looked momentarily troubled, but then seemed to make a quick recovery. "My dear, I'll talk with these young ladies. Perhaps you'd better return to your room." He went up a few steps, took her arm and managed to turn her around and head her up the stairs. When she had gone he came back down. "I must apologize for my wife's distracted mood," he said, still in a light friendly tone. "She has been under a great strain for some time."

Addie and Rose-Anne stared at him and finally Addie managed to ask, "How did you — I mean, were you expecting us?"

The man put his head back and laughed and it seemed to Addie a friendly sound. "We just rode through Barker Mills," he explained. "Two pretty young ladies passing through on a white horse and asking directions to the Drummond house didn't go unnoticed, let me tell you."

Addie repeated her introductions, which the man accepted with some gallantry and a small bow.

"Carlotta's girls," he murmured wonderingly. And then, more briskly, "And I am Abel Drummond; we're some kind of cousins, which I'm sure we can figure out in short order if we put our minds to it. Now come along and sit down. Take your bonnets off and make yourselves comfortable." He began motioning them into the tacky parlor through the archway to the right. "This is my business agent, Mr. Jonah

West." The girls nodded politely to the younger man, who was dark and stocky and had an outdoor look about him. They allowed themselves to be directed to chairs and sank down, and for the first time since they had left the Bowen troupe, Addie felt something like weakness and trembling come over her at the sheer lovely relief of being made welcome.

"You're very kind," she said rather unsteadily. "We surely do thank you."

"Now do I guess correctly," Abel Drummond went on gently, "that something has happened, some mischance, to bring you here?"

"You know about our mother, no doubt," Addie began, trying for firm tones but feeling suddenly emotional.

"Yes, yes, of course. Cousin Carlotta. Yes, I know of her passing. Your father sent us word. We were deeply grieved."

"We have now lost our father as well. He was killed in a fall only a week ago."

Abel Drummond looked genuinely shocked.

"Then you are quite alone in the world?"

"In a manner of speaking, Mr. Drummond. But all we want — "

"No, please, not 'mister'. We're cousins, you know."

"Thank you — Cousin Abel. All we want is to stay with you — with our grandfather — for a little while. There's no work till fall in the theater, you see. We have connections in New York and Philadelphia and a very good act of our own." She paused, thinking perhaps she had been unwise to speak of the theater so soon. A good many people disapproved of the stage and, after all, these relatives were

40

strangers to her. Perhaps when their mother had left this house it had been under some great cloud of family disapproval. But Abel Drummond took it all calmly.

"I'm sure you do," he said pleasantly. "I hope to see it one day. But in the meantime, you're to stay as long as you like."

Rose-Anne spoke for the first time, rather diffidently.

"That's more than kind of you, Cousin Abel. May we see our grandfather now?"

The smile on Abel Drummond's face faded. His mouth turned down sadly.

"I hope you can see him soon, my dear. Poor old gentleman; he's quite ill."

Addie let out an exclamation of dismay. Even though she had never met her grandfather, the news upset her. Thinking of him these past few days had made her feel less alone in the world. Abel Drummond looked at her sympathetically.

"It's been a long illness — over a year. My wife is quite exhausted with his care."

"We wouldn't want to disturb him," Addie said.

"Indeed not," Rose-Anne agreed with compassion.

"Hearing the news about your mother was a bitter blow to him. He's never been the same. But give me a little time to prepare him. We have to be cautious and slow in dealing with him."

"Oh, yes, please do," Rose-Anne begged. "I'd be so happy to help care for him."

Abel Drummond smiled at them both.

"What good kind girls you are," he said. "You're like your mother."

41

His gentleness and the gracious way he was receiving them touched Addie and made her realize how deep her own fears must have been. Even the news of their grandfather's illness, coming on the heels of the strange woman on the stairs, was not enough to unsettle her now. One thing at a time, she told herself sensibly. It will all work out. We have a safe place to stay.

She heard Rose-Anne asking, "He isn't going to die, is he?"

Addie's eyes went quickly to Abel Drummond, who hesitated for a moment before answering. Then he said quite simply, "Not as long as love and devotion can keep him alive." No one said anything for a little time and he went on in a brisker tone, "Well, now. Plenty of time for talk and getting acquainted later. You're here now and most welcome. I'm going to show you to your room and give you a chance to rest up."

What sort of accommodations would be available to travelers arriving unexpectedly, Addie wondered? Judging by the state of things on the first floor, the second floor might prove to be downright hazardous. Still, she and Rose-Anne had traveled enough and put up at enough out-of-the-way places to be prepared for anything.

"Oh — there's General Strong," she said suddenly, remembering. "We left our horse out in front."

"I'll look after him, Miss Trimble," said Jonah West, speaking for the first time.

"That's very kind of you," Addie said politely. She and Rose-Anne stood and prepared to follow their cousin upstairs. He was genial and talkative as he escorted them.

"It's a grand house, isn't it? Sturdy, well built. Your

grandfather built it himself. Burned the brick right here on the place. Oh, he had to hire masons and carpenters too, but he kept a sharp eye on everything and worked right along with them.

"This one's a corner room, bright and cheerful," he said, motioning expansively into the dusty gloom. "You make yourselves comfortable and ask for anything you need. Or better still, help yourselves. Don't be afraid to go right down to the kitchen. Mrs. Upjohn's in charge there and she'll see to whatever you need. We're just country folk here — live very simply — but I know you'll fit right in."

"Thank you very much, Cousin Abel," Addie said. "I'm sure everything will be just fine."

She glanced at Rose-Anne, silently prompting her to add her thanks, but Rose-Anne's eyes were going around the room with a look of stark disbelief. It was at least as bad as the parlor downstairs, and in addition smelled mustily of neglect and disuse. A cobweb that had caught them as they entered was draped across Rose-Anne's hair and she surveyed the room with dismay. But her expression turned serene as she spoke to Abel Drummond.

"There's just one thing, Cousin Abel," she said sweetly. "Above all, we don't want to be a nuisance. And you've had a great burden of illness which has been difficult for Mrs. Drummond — your wife, I mean."

"My wife's name is Caroline."

"Yes. Cousin Caroline. We wouldn't for the world add to that. So we must have your permission to — that is — to just dig in and help wherever anything needs doing about the household."

"Why, that's a very kind thought, my dear. And to be

sure, you need no permission whatever. You just dig right in." He repeated the phrase with some amusement. "If you find anything that needs doing, that is."

After they had closed the door on him they stood for a moment and finally Rose-Anne said in a weak voice, "If we find anything — "

"Oh, come now, my dear, it's just possible we may find something," Addie said archly.

"Some little thing."

"Yes, some trifle."

Rose-Anne went over and sat gingerly on the edge of the bed while Addie went to the window and carefully pulled back the dusty curtains.

"Pretty view," she observed. "Fields and trees. Once we clean the place up it won't be bad at all."

"Do we dare start right in on it? Would it look rude?"

"I don't think anybody would notice."

"Certainly Cousin Caroline wouldn't."

"About Cousin Caroline," Addie said, turning. "Were you thinking the same thing I was?"

"You mean about her taking care of Grandfather?"

Addie was glad Rose-Anne managed to think along the same lines she did. It saved a good many words.

"Yes. What kind of love and devotion can he be getting?"

"I thought that too. But perhaps Cousin Abel only said that to cover up. You know, because of the way she was. Maybe it's that woman in the kitchen — Mrs. Upjohn. Maybe she takes care of Grandfather."

"Why don't we go down and look her over?"

44

"She's probably the one in charge of buckets and mops anyway."

"It's like being in a strange country without a map," Addie commented.

"Only they're relatives, so we have to act as if we know what's going on. I don't even know who Cousin Abel is, do you?"

Addie nodded. "Mama spoke of him. He's her first cousin. I think he's lived here for some years helping Grandfather."

"Then that fellow who answered the door must be his son."

"I don't think so. I seem to remember Mama saying that Abel married late in life. I'll bet that's his stepson."

"He and his mother make a great pair."

"Like Tony Lumpkin and his ma in *She Stoops to Conquer.*"

Rose-Anne looked around the room thoughtfully. It was a spacious room, sparsely furnished country-fashion, with a bed, washstand, low chest and two straight chairs.

"Our mama never lived in this house, did she?"

"No. Grandfather was building it, she said, the year she went to Philadelphia. And of course she never came back."

This was a story they did know well. How their mother had come to study for a year at a young ladies' academy in Philadelphia under the chaperonage of a very proper Miss Pettibone and how Miss Pettibone had insisted on all her young ladies learning the newest dance steps. Mr. Terence Trimble, the handsome young dancing master, was in great demand that season, and there was scarcely a girl in

Philadelphia who was not making eyes at him. But it was the straight-backed little York Stater — that was how Terence had always referred to her — who caught his eye.

"I suppose there was a great row when she married Papa."

Addie shrugged. "I don't know. They never talked about that."

"Still, she never came back here."

"Well, maybe there was a row. Or maybe it was just that their lives changed so much. And being on the stage, you know, and having us, there couldn't have been much time for visiting."

They were silent for a moment. Then Rose-Anne said, "Cousin Abel seems kind."

Addie nodded. "I feel a little sorry for him, married to that woman and with that great oafish boy clumping around."

Rose-Anne, who always tried to be fair, said, "Of course one shouldn't make judgments on first impressions — "

"Oh, fiddle, why not? You saw what I saw."

They talked for a few more minutes before deciding to brave the kitchen. When they opened the door they found their two traveling bags standing outside in the hall and they guessed that Jonah West must have carried them up.

5

THE KITCHEN was an island, or perhaps more accurately a
fortress — a bastion set off from the rest of the house and
presided over by a ruddy, stout-armed chatelaine in the
person of Mrs. Upjohn. Pushing open the door timidly,
Addie and Rose-Anne exhaled with relief as they saw
shining pots and kettles, a huge scrubbed table, a chicken
freshly plucked and cleaned, a big bowl of brown and white
eggs. They would at least eat well while they were here.

"Good afternoon," Addie said. "Mrs. Upjohn?"

The woman behind the table waved a cleaver at them
and went to work on the chicken.

"How do, little ladies?" she shouted. "Come on in and
set. Mr. Abel Drummond told me about you. Glad you're
here. You'll be spending some time here in the kitchen, I
wouldn't doubt. Rest of the house is a pigsty anyway."

The girls exchanged startled glances as they came in and
sat on two wooden stools near the table.

47

"You the little granddaughters, eh? Ain't that nice. Ain't it just lovely. And been on the stage and all. My, you must've seen the sights. You can tell me all about it. Gets lonesome around here, lemme tell you. Nobody to talk to but her, and she ain't overly blessed with brains."

She jerked her head backward in the direction of an open door. Through it they could see into an adjoining room that seemed to be a summer kitchen. A servant girl with red hands and wrists was ironing there. She slanted them a sideways look and wiped her nose on the back of her hand.

"Lazy too," Mrs. Upjohn offered. "She's supposed to keep the rest of the house tidy, but she don't. Not that it matters much, for there wouldn't anybody notice if she did. *She* certainly can't be bothered lifting a finger," she added, rolling her eyes upward and leaving no doubt that *she* was Caroline Drummond.

"Do you have to cook special food for our Grandfather Drummond?" Addie asked. "Cousin Abel says he's quite ill."

"He's poorly, bless his dear heart, but I cook good strengthening things for him. This chicken's for some soup and I've got a custard in the oven out yonder." She jerked her head again in the direction of the summer kitchen. "Oh, I take good care of the old gentleman."

"I'm glad of that," Addie said, meaning it. "We'd carry his tray up for you, but Cousin Abel wants us to wait a bit before seeing him. He's fearful about too much excitement."

"Do tell. I'd think it would do him a world of good to see two such pretty faces."

"I guess there's more to it than that," Addie replied.

48

"Anyway, I can always find somebody to carry the tray up. Whoever's handy. I don't climb stairs myself. Haven't for years. I get the palpitations. Oh, if I had the strength, lemme tell you, I'd get after this place and knock her about the head for fair." The nod in the direction of the servant girl was an automatic thing. The girl seemed to pay no mind whatever.

Since there appeared to be no reason not to discuss the state of the house, Addie brought up what was on her mind.

"We thought perhaps you could give us buckets and rags, maybe a broom too, so we could clean up our room."

"Oh, to be sure, dearie. Anything you want. Right out there in the shed off the summer kitchen. We got rags by the bushel — ain't any of 'em used much," she added, raising her voice toward the servant girl.

The girl cast her a sullen look.

"And if you'd let us know what time supper is so we can tidy up and be ready — "

"Supper's at six. Anyways, that's when I put it on the table. You run down with your pitcher a few minutes before, I'll give you warm water for washin'. Or if I can stir that lout I'll get her to bring it to you."

"Oh, don't bother," Addie said hastily. "We'll come for it. Now — those cleaning rags are over here?"

"Ayuh. Right in there and through the door to the shed."

The two girls made their way into the summer kitchen, edging carefully around the board set up for ironing and nodding politely to the kitchen girl, who ignored them completely. The summer kitchen was as big as the main kitchen, with its own fireplace and bake ovens, its own big

49

work table. Many farmhouses had summer kitchens, either separated from the house or, like this one, adjoining, but Addie and Rose-Anne had never seen one so big and elaborate. It even had a plank floor and big open windows with no glass in them, but shutters for closing during cold or rainy weather. On a fine day like today the smell of honeysuckle came in through them, and the gentle sound of bees in the vines. A shed opened off this room, and even this was big and airy with shelves full of crocks and jars, with kegs and baskets and barrels. There were potatoes and carrots and turnips, apparently brought in from the root cellar and kept here in a handy place. There were onions hanging in knots from pegs on the walls. There was a big stoneware crock with more eggs. No matter how run-down the rest of the house might look, here in Mrs. Upjohn's domain there was order and plenty. Then the farm was being kept up even though the house was not, Addie thought.

The cook's voice followed after them.

"Big willow basket right there on the floor!" she sang out.

"We've found it," Addie called back. And they went to pick over the discarded rags which formed a small mountain in the outsized basket.

Rose-Anne went through them quickly, picking the right kind — soft for dusting, smooth for polishing. Rose-Anne was domestic by nature, quick and capable when it came to organizing a chore like this. But Addie was stayed by something else, and as Rose-Anne picked over the things critically Addie lifted a wrinkled petticoat and examined it. It was of fine thin lawn, carefully made and lace-trimmed. Its sole flaw seemed to be that it had a small rip in the hem

as though a heel had caught it there. She held it in one
hand and poked through the basket with the other, pulling
out a larger item — a dress of soft blue with a tiny collar
and pearl buttons down the bodice. It had a torn seam
under one sleeve. Addie had none of Rose-Anne's domestic
qualities — indeed, her sister's nesting tendencies disturbed
Addie at times, for it seemed totally unsuited to the theater
— but Addie was an expert seamstress. She made all their
costumes herself and often helped out others in the troupe
with their sewing. Now, looking over these discarded
clothes in the basket, her practiced eye assessed them with
astonishment. There was nothing wrong with them that an
evening's work couldn't set right. A few stitches here and
there, a bit of sponging, starching, ironing. And that blue
dress would look perfect on Rose-Anne. They must be from
Caroline Drummond's wardrobe.

"Rose-Anne," she whispered. "Look." She showed her
the dress and petticoat.

Rose-Anne's blue eyes widened. Neither she nor Addie
had ever had more than one everyday dress, one Sunday
dress and their costumes.

"Do we dare?" she asked, reacting as Addie had.

Addie made an abrupt decision.

"Certainly we dare. Anyway, it's nothing we're going to
keep secret. I'll tell Cousin Abel. Let's see what else is in
here." And now they began searching through the basket
more carefully. In the bottom was a rose-colored dress with
a torn collar and missing buttons, but otherwise whole.

"I'm sure they'd fit us," Addie whispered.

"They're elegant!"

In addition to the clothing there were sheets and

51

pillowslips — some showing signs of genuine wear, others with small three-cornered rips that wanted only simple patches. Over and over Addie shook her head at this prodigality, for the Trimbles had always been accustomed to efficiency, trim packing, careful mending.

They located buckets and brooms and went back up to their room, passing only long enough in the hallway outside their door to look at the other closed doors. There was no sound from behind any of them.

Rose-Anne struggled with the door catch and pushed into the room with the toe of one shoe. Where Addie had pulled the curtains back earlier there was now entering a shaft of bright dusty sunlight. It threw the untidiness and neglect of the place into sharper relief, but it offered too some promise of cheerfulness and light.

"It's not going to be half-bad," Rose-Anne commented, picturing the possibilities. She was looking flushed, even excited at the prospect of the siege.

Addie, who could never get worked up over housecleaning, grunted laconically. She dumped her bundle and set down her bucket of water.

"All right, Commodore, where do we start?"

They worked in their petticoats with their dresses laid out on the bed to keep them clean. Rose-Anne was in charge, directing the attack and deploying strength where it was most needed. They succeeded in forcing open a window so the sweet smells of the summer fields could enter, and as the afternoon wore away the room began to change gradually into a place of warmth and character. The windows shone with polishing, the floorboards gave back a soft glow where the sunlight struck them. Colors appeared, cobwebs vanished.

"It's beautiful," Rose-Anne breathed suddenly. "It's just beautiful."

"Well, at least it's clean," Addie puffed.

"And the whole house must be like this. Just think."

"Let's not think about it today," Addie said sharply. "I'm starved. Do you s'pose it's time to wash up?"

"I think it must be." Rose-Anne glanced at the lengthening shadows on the floor.

Addie went over to the bed and started putting on her dress. As she buttoned up the bodice she crossed to the washstand where the bowl and pitcher stood. She examined the pitcher.

"There's a spider in it," she said.

It seemed to Addie that mealtime in the Drummond house was, if this first evening was any example, a haphazard affair. Only the four of them — Addie, Rose-Anne, Abel Drummond and Jonah West — sat down to eat in the dining room. Abel Drummond had taken a tray up to old Jeremiah himself, and there had been not a word or sign from Caroline Drummond. The young man in the clumping shoes, who had been introduced to them as Philip Hess and who was indeed Abel's stepson, had eaten ahead of the rest of them, sitting at the kitchen table and conversing with Mrs. Upjohn. Then, wiping his mouth on his sleeve, he had left the house again, headed toward the barn.

"Philip keeps very busy around the place," Abel Drummond explained calmly as they sat down to eat. None of this catch-as-catch-can aspect of the household seemed to bother him in the least. Either he was so used to it that he

53

no longer noticed or else he was making a determined and skillful effort to overlook it. Addie wondered if Caroline Drummond's state today was her usual one or whether they had happened to arrive at a time of particular crisis.

The supper was good — simple country cooking but plentiful. Addie found herself astonishingly hungry but ate carefully, not wanting to terrify her cousin with the prospect of two greedy boarders. Conversation came quite easily. Out of deference to the girls there was considerable talk of the theater, on which subject both men were fairly knowledgeable. Abel Drummond had seen Edmund Kean play Shylock, and Addie admitted that Portia's courtroom speech was one she had conned herself to do as a reading between acts when a fill-in was needed. She was delighted to be in the company of people who had at least seen New York and Philadelphia, and it made the prospect of their being stranded here temporarily a little less bleak.

Then, when they were finishing she said, "Cousin Abel, we asked Mrs. Upjohn for cleaning rags this afternoon and among them we found some clothing, quite good but in need of mending. May we have it?" She spoke very directly, feeling there was no reason to try to hide their reduced circumstances.

Abel Drummond flushed with color and looked uncomfortable.

"Why, to be sure, my dear. Yes, of course, anything you find. It's perfectly all right. Only — if you need something, let me bring you some lengths of new cloth from the town. They receive goods from New York and Albany quite often."

Addie shook her head.

"No," she said carefully. "Thank you very much, but these will do nicely." Not too much too fast, she was thinking. Wait and see how things stand here. "I only wanted to ask if it was all right. I wanted to be sure Mrs. — Cousin Caroline wouldn't mind."

"No, indeed. She'll be most happy for you to make use of them," he said.

After the candle was blown out in their room that night, Addie knelt by the window, her arms folded on the sill, looking out. Rose-Anne called sleepily to her from the bed.

"Addie, aren't you worn out? Come to bed."

"I will. Right away. I just want to look out for a minute."

"Wish I could've washed the bedding. But I will, tomorrow." Rose-Anne's voice was growing thready. "Curtains too, and beat the rug — "

Presently Addie could hear her breathing deepen into sleep.

It was odd, Addie reflected, that this afternoon when she had looked out in broad sunlight, she had noticed only fields and barns. Now that she looked by moonlight, it all took on more character and everything seemed clearer, all outlines sharpened by shadow. She could see the fields, sloping back gently toward barns. One barn was smaller and made of logs. The larger one was of cut lumber. She supposed that had been built later. And there were any number of smaller buildings — sheds and coops, she supposed. She knew very little of farm life. Then the fields continued on back and sloping upward gently to a point where they seemed to touch a rim of trees. This wooded part rose more steeply, and that was where the plow had stopped. But that was to the left. To the right it was open land and the slope fell away into a kind of hollow or perhaps a creek bottom. She could see something gleam silver there and she guessed it might be a little pond or a marshy place where the cattle went. It might be fun, she thought, to walk about tomorrow and see what it all looked like. The whole trick to getting along anyplace, she reasoned, was not to fight it. Now this was not the place she would have picked to stay, of course, but there were advantages. They had been welcomed and there was plenty of food and no more worries until fall, when they could move on. There would be ample time for her to work on a new act, open country where she and Rose-Anne could rehearse without bothering anybody. All in all, they could count themselves fortunate in just having a place to go. And if she were going to worry about anything, it certainly should not be this little summertime interlude which would not hurt either of them. The bigger worry was over what would happen in the autumn and where they would get work. Who would hire them? What theater people did she know or had she heard her father speak of? Maybelle and Billy would help, she was sure —

Addie's thoughts stopped with an abrupt thump of her heart. Someone was outside there, moving around. She watched, holding her breath, as a figure moved slowly and steadily up from the little creek hollow, a small thin figure in a long dark cloak that reached to the ground. Sometimes the figure paused and bent over as though searching for something.

Addie leaned forward a little. She could hear a sound, thin and distant. Not exactly singing — more like a droning noise, a tuneless kind of song. She felt a chill and the small hairs along her arms prickled up.

The figure advanced, still bending now and then. It stood midway between the two barns and the house and in the light of the nearly full moon Addie could see it plainly, although the face was in shadow, partly covered by a hood. And now the person stood quite still. Whoever it was looked up at the open window. Addie shrank back into the shadows.

Looked at her.

6

BREAKFAST the following morning was no better organized than supper had been, but it was not set in the dining room, so it had a friendlier, more informal quality. Mrs. Upjohn put everything out on the big kitchen table and each new arrival helped himself. It seemed a good system, given the independent spirit of this odd household, where an every-man-for-himself attitude seemed to prevail.

And Mrs. Upjohn, who complained about everything else, at least enjoyed her cooking. She made countless trips back and forth from summer kitchen to table with big slabs of toasted bread on a fork, with cheese, porridge and tea. Her sleeves were rolled up over her stout forearms, her broad face reddened with exertion. With every trip she managed to rail in a routine way at the kitchen girl, who this morning had been set to kneading dough for a new baking of bread.

"Keep at it, girl, that ain't near done!" she shouted. "Punch it in!"

She brought Addie and Rose-Anne fresh toast with cheese melting off the edges and said boldly, "Saw you carryin' quite a load of duds upstairs yestiddy. Goin' to sew 'em up, are you?"

"Our cousin, Mr. Abel Drummond, said we might," Addie replied with some dignity. Yet she did not resent Mrs. Upjohn's prying, since it was so good-natured.

"Well, good. Go to it, I say. Ain't a place you could turn in this house that wouldn't be better for the needle or the broom, but who's to do it I couldn't say."

Rose-Anne took a bite of her toast and a swallow of tea and said thoughtfully, "I wanted to ask you about that, Mrs. Upjohn. Would anyone mind if I cleaned up the house a bit?"

Addie glared at her, but Mrs. Upjohn's loud hoot of laughter stopped her from commenting.

"Lord save us, girl," the woman shouted. "You'd have to start with a shovel."

"I know that," Rose-Anne said, "but it's a lovely house and I'd like to see it looking right. And I haven't anything to take up my time. I'd be glad to do it."

Addie went on eating, making no comment although it riled her more than a little to hear Rose-Anne go on like that. She had never approved of this domestic side of her sister — this nesting instinct that seemed always just beneath the surface. It was, Addie considered, a danger to be guarded against. With Rose-Anne's slim golden beauty, her grace, her talent, she was born for the stage. Addie certainly did not want her busying herself the whole summer with buckets and mops.

"Why, my stars, love, you just go right to it," Mrs. Upjohn

said heartily. "I couldn't promise anybody around here would thank you for it or even notice you done it, but if it would give you pleasure, go to it."

"And I'd like to help you here in the kitchen too," Rose-Anne said. "Back home in Philadelphia we live in Mrs. Brindley's boarding house. It's near the theater and it's very friendly. But we don't get into the kitchen often. I'd like to know how to cook and — oh, so many things. Maybe you could teach me and then I could be of some help too."

Mrs. Upjohn stared at her, melting as people always melted in the face of Rose-Anne's innocence.

"Why, bless your heart, dearie," she said. "You just come ahead any time and make yourself right to home here."

Addie felt a rather desperate need to stanch this flood of domesticity.

"Perhaps you should ask permission of our cousin Mrs. Drummond," she said primly. "It might be she'd want to be consulted."

"Oh, her!" Mrs. Upjohn hooted. "Lord save us, *she'd* never care — " She broke off and grabbed a pitcher. "Cream for your tea, Miss?" she asked formally as the kitchen door opened and Caroline Drummond entered.

Addie and Rose-Anne got up from the table and stood politely.

"Good morning," they both said.

"Please sit down and go on with your breakfast," the woman said, waving a thin hand at them. "I'll have tea, Steadfast."

Addie and Rose-Anne refrained from looking at each

other. Steadfast Upjohn was too incredible a name to contemplate together.

"Right away, Ma'am," the woman said, putting out a fresh cup and pouring the tea.

Caroline Drummond took a seat opposite the girls and sank down, propping her elbows on the table and resting her head in her hands for a moment. Then she gave a loud sigh and straightened herself.

"Has that tea been steeping for more than five minutes?" she asked sharply.

"No, indeed, Ma'am, I just set it out," Mrs. Upjohn insisted, and Addie and Rose-Anne chimed in awkwardly, affirming that it was certainly delicious. Caroline Drummond took the cup in both hands and drank. When she set it down she looked across the table and said, "I hope you've been able to make yourselves comfortable here."

"Oh, we have. Yes, Ma'am," Addie replied quickly. "We do thank you and Cousin Abel for being so kind as to take us in." She said it because it seemed the correct thing — to get off on the right foot, so to speak. But underneath a small nudging thought reminded her that it was their grandfather's house after all and that they had every right to be here.

Yet Caroline Drummond seemed in her offhand way not to mind their presence.

"Oh, it's all right — " She waved a hand vaguely and drank more tea. Her eyes moved restlessly around the kitchen and her hands were never still. They plucked at the blue and white tablecloth, picked up a spoon and put it down, tapped on her saucer. She must have been quite a

61

beauty at one time, perhaps when Abel Drummond married her, Addie thought. She had large dark eyes, a full sensitive mouth, an elegant broad forehead. But there were lines at the corners of her mouth and eyes that seemed to pull her whole face downward into a look of discontent. She had an aimless, undirected air, as though she needed someone to pull her together, tell her what to do next. Yet one did not command Caroline Drummond, Addie guessed. She was dressed, despite the heat of the summer morning, in a wrapper of rich green velvet and her dark hair, which showed only here and there a strand of gray, was twisted up into a hasty knot that was for all its carelessness becoming.

"I was just telling Mrs. Upjohn," Rose-Anne said shyly, "that I'd be happy to help with the housework while we're here — uh — Cousin Caroline."

"Hah. No one's going to thank you for it," Caroline Drummond said scornfully. How odd, Addie thought, that it was just what Mrs. Upjohn had said, but when Caroline said it the meaning seemed different. "No one cares what gets done around here. Middle of nowhere," she added aimlessly, reaching up to tuck back a strand of hair. "I've been used to city living myself."

"Oh, is that so?" Addie asked.

"Yes. I'm from Philadelphia."

"Indeed? That's where we're from."

Caroline Drummond seemed to have to pull herself back to them to remind herself they were there. She frowned, trying to think of something.

"Yes. You're — what is it — on the stage?"

"Yes, we are. Our whole family were theater people,"

Addie said proudly. The pride crept in because she was not sure whether there was criticism or perhaps condescension in the woman's tone. But again there seemed to be neither, merely indifference.

"I used to enjoy the theater — " Caroline began, but her voice trailed off.

"We plan to return to it very soon," Addie said, directing this remark as much to Rose-Anne. Then, trying a different approach, she said, "We hope it won't be long before we'll be allowed a little visit with our grandfather. We wouldn't want to tax him, of course — "

There was a sound at the back door and the young man Philip Hess came in bearing a huge basket of red raspberries. His look glanced off the three at the table quickly and went to Mrs. Upjohn.

"Use these, can you?" he asked.

Mrs. Upjohn put her hands on her hips and looked heavenward for aid.

"On baking day! Lord save us, Philip." Her tone with him was easy and familiar. "You'll have me jumpin' like spit on a hot skillet, the work you're handin' me. Well, I'll whack up some biscuits for shortcake — use the oven as long's I've got it hot anyway. But all them — " She shook her head. "What'd you ever pick 'em all for today? I thought you were still cutting hay."

"I didn't," Philip said crossly. "*He* picked 'em. Well, I'll leave 'em here."

"Oh, but — " Rose-Anne jumped to her feet. "It's so warm today and if they're just left won't they spoil? I mean, those on the bottom will get soft, won't they?"

Philip Hess stopped and turned to look at her. He flushed

63

at being addressed directly, but he did not answer — merely shrugged his shoulders. Rose-Anne appealed to Mrs. Upjohn.

"If you weren't so busy, Mrs. Upjohn, what would you do with them? I mean, to keep them?"

"Why, make raspberry jam is what I'd do. But it's a whole afternoon's work, that many berries. The preserve glasses all got to be washed, and then the preserves got to be waxed over once you've made 'em. And it's a hot afternoon's stirrin', lemme tell you."

"I could do it," Rose-Anne said eagerly. "You just tell me how and I'll do it. It would be dreadful to waste them."

"Well — " Mrs. Upjohn hesitated, then shrugged. "You can if you're a mind to, dearie. My, but you surely are the least little mite of a thing to have all that starch."

"You don't mind, do you, Cousin Caroline?" Rose-Anne asked.

Caroline Drummond shrugged her shoulders and drank her tea.

"Just as you like," she said indifferently.

Philip put the big basket down on the floor by the door and turned to go.

"Oh, Philip!" Caroline Drummond's voice stopped her son before he could get through the door. It seemed to Addie his back stiffened as he paused. When he turned back into the room his face had a closed look. He was not an ill-favored young man, Addie thought. His hair was dark and strong-looking like his mother's. He had her large dark eyes. His mouth was wide, his chin square. Not ill-favored at all. But so dark, so glowering, so rigid. Did he ever smile, she wondered?

64

The woman at the table moved her hands in a restless appealing gesture, turning them palms up.

"Why don't you stop and have some tea with me?" Not with us, Addie noticed.

"I've had my breakfast, Mother. And I'm busy. I have men haying today. I have to join them."

"That could wait, couldn't it? Or couldn't someone else — "

"Who?" he exploded, so violently that Addie and Rose-Anne both jumped. "Who'll do it if I don't?" And he strode out angrily, out into the summer sunshine of the farmyard. Addie, who had been on the point of asking about General Strong and where he had been quartered, was glad she had kept silent.

She glanced curiously at the basket Philip had left behind. The berries were mounded up in it like piles of soft red velvet. *He* had picked them, Philip Hess said. Who was *he*, Addie wondered? A hired man perhaps?

For a moment no one said anything. Because the young man's tone had been so angry it had left an uncomfortable pall behind. But Caroline Drummond showed little reaction other than to look about the room with darting glances of her dark eyes.

"Still, there's no reason why we can't sit down to a civilized dinner at noon, is there?" she asked. She did not direct the remark at anyone in particular and Addie wondered if a reply was expected of her.

Mrs. Upjohn stepped in with a conciliatory tone.

"Why, no, Ma'am. No reason. If you'll tell me what you'd like. The only thing is, Mr. Drummond and Mr. West have ridden out for the whole day. And Mr. Philip will be taking his nooning in the field with the men." The relationship between the two women seemed an odd one, Addie thought, for although Mrs. Upjohn treated Caroline Drummond with proper courtesy, servant to mistress, still it was apparent that she felt only contempt for her. And it seemed too that in any question of decision-making or authority on household matters she was the final word, so that the business of giving orders and planning procedure was probably only a sort of act, a routine they went through.

"Oh, well, what's the use!" Caroline Drummond shouted, pushing back from the table and getting to her feet. "I don't know why I even try!" And without another word she swept from the room.

Mrs. Upjohn shrugged and cleared away the empty cup and saucer. Addie said nothing. It would be getting off on the wrong foot altogether, she felt, to ask questions or engage in kitchen gossip, but she did feel a sense of pity for Abel Drummond. And again she thought about her grandfather, old Jeremiah Drummond, lying upstairs old and sick, dependent on the hit-or-miss ministrations of a slovenly servant girl and whatever other chance attention he might be lucky enough to receive. Abel's concern about not upsetting their grandfather was genuine enough, Addie was sure, but was it good sense? She and Rose-Anne could do so much for the old man if only they were allowed to.

"Mrs. Upjohn, which room upstairs is our grandfather's?" she asked suddenly.

"Up the backstairs, dearie. First door you come to."

Rose-Anne glanced at Addie curiously but said nothing. Shortly afterward Addie left the kitchen, with Rose-Anne and Mrs. Upjohn still at the big table in a welter of culinary enthusiasm. Their voices followed her out into the hall.

"What's a nooning, Mrs. Upjohn?"

"Why, that's when the men take their noon meal out in the field, is all. We'll have to pack a stout basket, lemme tell you. There's four of 'em haying today, counting Mr. Philip. Mix up a jug of switchel too."

"What's switchel?"

"Glory be, you are a city girl, ain't you? Why, it's water, molasses, a little bit of sweet vinegar and some ginger. We'll fill that jug there — "

"This one?"

"No, t'other one next to it, for it's got the least little bit of a leak. You put switchel in a jug with a leak on a hot day, it keeps cooler. Not a big leak, mind you — "

Addie went up the backstairs feeling suddenly rather lonely.

These steps were narrower but no less carefully finished than the front stairs. The treads showed considerably more wear, however. At the top was a narrow hallway, an offshoot of the open main hallway that was built around the big center staircase. Doors opened off this narrow passageway to right and left, and she could see how the first room at the top of the stairs would be handy as quarters for an invalid, since trays could be carried up and down easily. She paused in front of it and even reached out to touch the smooth white-painted door with the palm of her hand. Hearing Rose-Anne chatting happily with Mrs. Upjohn in the kitchen downstairs had made her feel adrift, unconnected, unbelonging. She longed to establish contact with somebody, to explain why she had come here. But after a moment she let her hand drop and went on down the hall toward her own room. It would not do to rush things.

Once in the bedroom she set about finding tasks to turn her hand to. She took out her sewing things and set to work on the dresses and petticoat she had salvaged, but it was simple mending and was finished in a half-hour. The things needed no more than a bit of airing out in the sun and perhaps a touch of the iron. She could do that this afternoon. She put her needle, thread and thimble away and sat looking around the room. The sun was streaming in, bright and reassuring. The birds and insects outside were busy with songs and talk that came in through the window.

Addie felt her eyes filling up with slow misty tears. She would have given anything right at that moment for the sound of Terence's voice. *Come on, darlin', look sharp, we're on!* It took her a minute to get hold of herself. Now that will be all of that, she told herself firmly. If you are sniveling and moping for the sight of a familiar face, go visit General Strong. And she had to laugh at the thought of the General's long sweet face, his wistful look as he waited for an apple. There must be apples down in that shed, she thought.

7

SHE FOUND the General in the company of another horse and five red and white cows in a far sloping corner of pasture near the line where the trees started. It was a high windy spot with good shade at its edges and with plenty of grass and field flowers. As she climbed up she could see General Strong cropping the grass with his long neck stretched low. He heard her step, raised his head and came hurrying over to the log fence to greet her. There was no mistaking his pleasure in seeing her, and the apple delighted him even though it was from last fall and quite withered. But then the second horse came over to join them, an ancient sway-backed beast with a plain homely face that looked so wistful at the sight of the General chomping juicily on the apple that Addie was sorry she had brought only one. She patted the old horse and explained it to him. The two horses stayed at the fence with her for a time but then the old one turned to go back to the shade and the General followed after. So even the General has found a friend, Addie thought.

She hitched herself up so she could sit on the top fence rail and looked down over the long slope toward the rest of the farm. She could see the house and pick out her own window. She could see down across the little hollow where she had noticed the strange hooded figure in the night. There was indeed a small stream meandering there, just as she had suspected. And beyond, in a farther field, she could see the figures of four men cutting hay with scythes. They moved together, all in a line, keeping their distance from each other and their strokes together. One of them was the city-bred Philip Hess, she thought idly, whose mother did not want him to be a farmer. From this far you could never pick him out though. Give him credit for being a hard worker anyway. You would certainly never cast him in a role requiring charm, but he was not afraid of work. She watched the line of mowers for a long time, thinking it a brave sight.

Finally she slid off the fence and called good-bye to the General, promising that she would try to come again the next day. Instead of heading back toward the house she turned and followed along the rail fence in the other direction, up through the sloping pasture, cutting diagonally across the hill and around it to the other side. She was warm and a little winded by the time she reached the far side. When she looked down she was surprised to see that she was on a faint narrow path that wound through the field. An animal track or footpath it seemed to be, but the odd thing was that she did not remember where it had started or how she had come upon it. Still, there it was, making the walking easier, so she followed it down through the meadow and into a field that was considerably lower, flatter and boggier than the one she had just left. Far off to the right in a corner of the field stood a little log house. That was where the path seemed to end.

She was certain she was still on Drummond property so she had no qualms about exploring. Someone must live in the little house — some tenant or hired hand — but she would not intrude or make a nuisance of herself, merely offer a good-day-to-you and go on with her walk. Yet a strange thing happened as she made her way down the steep slope and across the field, following the turns and curves of the little path. The sun, which had been high and bright before, became lost behind a thick gray cloud. The wind, which had been warm and lively, turned chilly. Little black flies buzzed annoyingly around her head and she could feel the ground beneath her feet turning uncomfortably soft and giving way with each step she took.

She was reassured as she drew nearer the place. It was a snug-looking house with a well-tended vegetable garden alongside it. Some country wife must put in long hours on that, she guessed. And there was, her nose told her, an herb garden too. After a moment she spotted it, a green and fragrant patch near the door, the various herbs separated from one another by rows of stones to keep sage from mixing with savory, marjoram with mint. Three trees stood a little back from the house, making pleasant shaded spots. Addie was not an expert on trees, but she guessed them to be alder, willow and elder.

She was near enough to hear the hum of the bees in the

71

mint bed when she saw the other garden patch. It lay beyond the vegetables, past the corner of the house, and a more ugly tangle of plants Addie had never seen. They grew in profusion — twisting, pushing, writhing about one another. Some were bushy with drooping bell-shaped flowers of dull bluish purple. Some had pallid yellow fruit and one, which grew as high as Addie's waist, had sticky hairy leaves veined with purple. She could discern now among the fresh herb and garden scents a strong sickly odor that she was sure must come from this patch. Why on earth, she wondered with a frown, would any good farm woman cultivate things like that?

She raised her hand and gave a knock at the door. There was no sound from inside. She started to knock again, only this time she hesitated and stood there poised, her knuckles curved toward the rough-hewn wood. Something came to her — a sudden knowledge that there was someone behind her. She turned around slowly.

Her heart gave a thump that sent it leaping right into her throat as she saw the man standing there. Or no, perhaps not a man. Perhaps a boy. He had a broad powerful build, but it was somehow contradicted in his face, which had a childlike vacancy. His mouth was slightly open and the eyes that were staring at her carried no expression behind them. A loony, Addie thought, feeling panicky. Not right in the head. What would she do now? Almost at once the door behind her opened.

"Yes? Well?" It was a sharp querulous voice that seemed to hold annoyance.

Addie turned back. The woman standing in the open doorway was short and slight, wearing a long dress of

72

shapeless black. Gray hair was knotted up tightly on the top of her head but a wisp straggled lankly down at each side of her face. She had a prominent curving nose and black darting eyes that seemed to burn intensely.

I've seen you before, Addie said silently.

Aloud she said, "How do you do?" but her voice was not quite steady. She was beginning to feel this whole walk had been a mistake. It was one of those situations which took yards and yards of explanation and in the long run were not worth the trouble. Before she could even start, however, the woman spoke up.

"You're too early, girl. I told you sundown, didn't I? 'Tisn't near ready. Besides — " The sharp eyes went over Addie critically. "Where's the eggs?"

"Eggs?" Addie echoed the word blankly.

"A dozen eggs is what I said." The woman shook her head as though exasperated. "You girls are all alike. You think I can just make these things up in a wink. It takes some doing, you know. Why, I was out last night at midnight gathering thistles. It's no good, you know, except just before the moon's full, and with the left hand too, which takes a while."

Addie was bewildered, but she was also annoyed at the woman's berating her.

"Look here," she said, "I'm just out for a walk. I don't know anything about any eggs, or thistles either."

"Ain't you Essie?" the woman asked, frowning. She shaded her eyes and looked more closely. "Ain't you the Drummonds' kitchen girl?"

"No, I'm not," Addie replied in icy tones, not at all flattered at the confusion.

73

"Light's poor here," the woman mumbled. "Who are you then?"

"I'm a guest at the Drummond house," Addie said with dignity. "My name's Adelina. And I was just taking a walk."

"Nothing better to do?"

"Well — " It seemed to Addie this was a very odd conversation, and she was aware, all the time, of deep heavy breathing behind her. "I come out to see my horse. He's up in that high pasture."

The old eyes narrowed.

"That white horse? He yours?"

"Yes, he is."

For some reason this seemed to weigh in Addie's favor. The woman hesitated for another minute and then stepped back, opening the door a little wider.

"Come inside," she said. Addie supposed it was an invitation, but it sounded more like an order. She hesitated. "Come on, come on!" the woman shouted. "Bees'll be comin' in if you don't. No, now you stay there. I'll tell you about it later," she said crossly. Addie thought she was addressing the strange boy, but she seemed to be looking at the mint patch where the bees circled and hummed. Addie glanced nervously over her shoulder and found the vacant eyes still on her.

"You get back to your chores," the woman ordered the boy, and he walked off with a shambling loose-armed gait. His hands, hanging slack at his sides, seemed to bear pinkish stains. Raspberries? Addie wondered. The woman had gone into the dimness of the little house so there seemed nothing for Addie to do but follow. She could not say that she was afraid, exactly. She was, after all, scarcely out of sight of her grandfather's house. But something about the situation was uncomfortable.

"Staying at the big house, are you," the woman said in a thoughtful way. "Well, now." She closed the door behind Addie, who stood there getting used to the dimness, for only a small amount of light came in through the little window. It was cold too, Addie noticed, in spite of the warmth of the summer day. The cabin was tiny and seemed to have only one room, although she could see an adjoining woodshed. There was a fireplace with a fire laid in it, but it was completely dark and cold. Well, that was not strange, Addie reasoned. Since it was summer they more than likely cooked over an outdoor fire.

The woman went to a good-sized table that stood in the middle of the one small room. She had a number of bowls and pots ranged on it along with a large mortar and a pestle. While Addie stood there uncertainly she began grinding and mixing, obviously taking up a job that Addie's arrival had interrupted. Addie looked around. There was very little in the room except for the table, which was so large it seemed to take almost the whole area. Against one wall was crowded a narrow pallet — the dimwitted boy must sleep in the shed, Addie surmised — and there were two straight chairs jammed against the wall. Everything else seemed to be on the wall. There were hooks, pegs, racks, shelves, and everything was full. Scraps of clothing hung from the pegs, pots and kettles and cups from the hooks. And every shelf was loaded, chiefly with stoneware crocks of every imaginable size and shape — some as small as teacups, some as big as a two-gallon measure. No two seemed to be alike. Many of them were labeled in an uncertain hand and with lavish use of abbreviations: "sage," "savory," "tarr.," "bay," "dill," "rosem." Those were easy to figure out. But another group on a higher shelf puzzled her. There she saw "hen.," "hem.," "n.sh.," "m.dr.," "w.b." The writing was scraggly and done in something darkly purplish. Pokeberry juice, Addie guessed.

"They're always rushing me," the woman complained, grinding furiously. "I don't know when they think I catch up on my sleep. Most of these things have to be picked at midnight, or thereabouts."

"Yes, I think I saw you last night," Addie said boldly.

The woman gave her a sharp look.

"In the window, were you? Ayuh, I saw you too." And she looked at Addie quite intently. Then she went back to her job. "Four good thistles is what I was looking for."

"Did you find them?"

"I did. And of course the beanflowers I picked in May. Keep those on hand all the time — dried."

"What are the four thistles for?" Addie inquired, beginning to understand at last what it was all about but wanting to be sure.

"The girl puts those at the four corners of her pillow tonight. Gives 'em each a name — of some feller, you know? Then whichever one grows a fresh sprout in the night, that's the one for her. So she gives him the potion. Ain't anything stronger than beanflower potion, you know, to fetch a young man."

Addie let her breath out, releasing some of the tension she had been feeling since she stepped into this odd situation. She smiled but took care not to laugh outright, since it was obvious the woman was quite serious about her work. These old grannies were quite a common thing; Addie had often heard of them. They gathered herbs and roots and flowers and mixed up harmless love potions for silly servant girls.

"Of course that ain't anywheres near all I do," the old woman said as if reading her thoughts. "I do simpling too."

"Is that so?" Addie inquired politely.

"Oh, to be sure. I mix remedies for pretty near anything you could name — dropsy, consumption, liver complaint, weak heart, falling sickness."

"Goodness!" Addie recalled the strange garden patch. "Those plants outside, back at the corner there. Are those some of your medicines?"

The pestle stopped its pounding and the old woman's head, which had been bent over her work, came up slowly.

"Some of 'em, ayuh," she answered.

Addie shivered and crossed her arms in front of her, rubbing them suddenly to warm up.

"Feel a chill, do ye?" the woman inquired.

"Oh, no. Goodness, it's a very warm day," Addie replied hastily. But she was chilly.

The old woman looked over her shoulder at the dark fireplace, staring at it for a long moment. Then she turned back to her job.

"How's old mister?" she asked abruptly.

The question surprised Addie at first, but then she realized that this woman must have lived here for years and, in the manner of old country folk, probably knew all the business of the big household. She had, in any case, a handy supplier of information in the person of Essie, the kitchen

77

girl. And a handy supplier of eggs too, Addie thought with some amusement. She wondered how that was getting by Mrs. Upjohn.

"I haven't seen him since I came here," she said, choosing her words carefully.

"Be you kin?" the woman asked, not at all daunted.

"Only distantly," Addie hedged.

Once again the old woman studied her closely, but she only grunted.

"How do they call you again?" she asked.

"Adelina. Addie, they call me mostly."

"I'm called Florinda," the woman offered. "It's got to do with flowers."

Addie bobbed a small curtsy.

"Do ye know the language of the flowers?" the woman asked.

"No, I'm afraid I don't."

"The flowers hold their secrets," Florinda said darkly. "There's meaning there."

"Yes, I suppose so. I just know things like rose or lily." Something popped into Addie's head. Sad lines from *Hamlet* — something about Ophelia, it was. *There with fantastic garlands did she come, of crow-flowers, nettles, daisies and long purples.* "Do you know about crow-flowers, nettles, daisies and long purples?" she asked, smiling a little and half-joking.

But Florinda's hand jerked and the pestle clacked against the mortar.

"Lord, girl, what makes you ask such things?"

"I just heard of them somewhere," Addie said vaguely. "There was a girl who — "

"Well, don't have 'em around you," Florinda interrupted sternly. "Not all in a bunch, that is. One at a time, maybe, wouldn't hurt."

"Why? What do you mean?"

The woman raised a hand and named them on crooked fingers.

"Crow-flowers, that stands for a fair maid. Nettles means stung to the quick. Daisies means youthful bloom. Long purples — they call those Dead Men's Fingers — that means under the cold hand of death."

Addie swallowed, thinking of poor Ophelia drowned in the stream.

"Mercy," she murmured. She looked around her at the laden shelves with all their labeled crocks. "Do you grow all these things yourself?"

"Some. And some just grows wild, but I mind where to seek 'em out."

"What about those on that high shelf? I can't read what they say."

The woman shifted about behind the table, making fussy motions with her hands and locating a fresh bunch of dried flowers to add to her mixture.

"Angelica," she said, indicating the gray green sprigs she held. "I generally put in a little, even though 'tisn't called for. There ain't anything you can brew up that a little angelica doesn't improve it. It's a holy plant; it wards off evil."

Addie realized that she was evading the question.

"Are those special medicines up there?" she persisted.

"Yes. Special." Florinda held the little bunch of angelica tightly in front of her and raised her eyes to the shelf where the jars bore the cryptic abbreviations. "Henbane," she said, reciting in a hollow tone, "hemlock, nightshade, mandrake, wolfbane — "

"Aren't those poisons?" Addie asked sharply.

"Some say they be."

"Well, aren't they?"

"Kill or cure. Cure or kill."

Addie smelled smoke.

"I think something's burning," she said.

The woman did not answer. She had returned to her mixing. Behind her in the cold fireplace a wisp of white smoke curled up around a log. While Addie stared, an orange flame licked up after it, sending it up the chimney in a puff. The flame wound itself around the log, grew and crackled. Within moments a fire was starting up.

"That's funny," Addie said slowly. "I wouldn't have thought there were any live coals in there at all."

"The eyes don't see all." Florinda's sepulchral tone had vanished. Now it was dry and curt.

Addie moved her feet uneasily.

"I think I'd best be going," she said. She was feeling a little nervous, off balance. An air of unreality seemed to close in around her in the strange house and she did not care for it. She was not, like the egg-stealing Essie, a simple country girl who believed she could catch a young man with dried beanflowers, but something in the atmosphere of this place chilled her, something half-expressed, not quite understood.

Florinda made no objection, but she said, "Take old mister some elixir. I've mixed it up for him."

80

"I probably won't be seeing him right away," Addie hedged.

"Then give it to that fool in the kitchen."

"Well, I don't know if Mrs. Upjohn would — " Addie began, and then she thought, oh, take it. What harm can it do to carry it back with you? "All right."

"It's for times when he feels poorly or faint," Florinda explained. "My special foxglove tonic, and I made it with a good deal of care. Gathered the leaves myself with the left hand and from the north side of the hedge. That's important. And I put in a little sage too. That's for long life."

She bustled to the mantel and took down a small earthenware cruet with a cork stopper.

"There."

Addie took it. The smooth surface felt cold in her hands.

"Now mind he takes it," the woman said sharply.

"I'll do my best," Addie lied.

"Now about that girl — " Florinda said thoughtfully.

"Essie?"

"No, no." She brushed Essie aside. "That other one you asked me about. The one who was gathering those flowers."

Ophelia? Addie thought dizzily.

"Well, she wasn't gathering them exactly. I think she was wearing them."

"Wearing! Oh, then likely it's too late. I thought maybe you could tell her to gather up some angelica and even some purple mallow to offset them."

"No, I'm afraid it is too late."

The woman looked at her accusingly. "You should've come to me sooner. I'd've told you."

"Well. Good day," Addie murmured, ducking out through the door.

She hurried along the path that crossed the meadow and wound up the slope. She had never, even on the stage, felt more a part of a make-believe situation than she did at this moment. She felt like laughing and crying at the same time — it had been so funny, yet not altogether funny. One thing she was positive of: She was not going to let her grandfather taste any of this whatever-it-was elixir. She lifted the cork and sniffed. A thin bitter smell wafted out. She waited till she was out of sight of the little log house and then poured the liquid out on the ground. She was quite sure no one saw her do it.

8

It was not, Addie decided after their first few days there, the worst thing that could have happened to them. Taken all in all, it had worked out passably well, their coming to their grandfather's farm. She was even beginning to get used to it, and to the odd assortment of people that made up the household. They were totally unlike anyone she had grown up with. At the boarding house in Philadelphia, or in the theater, the people she had known best were emotional, dramatic, warm, spiteful or grudging — sometimes a mixture of all these things. Whatever they were, they were easy to know and understand. The people here were different. They had an odd way of talking past each other in oblique sentences that were sometimes left unfinished. They seemed, more often than not, wrapped up in existences of their own, looking inward. There was almost no way, for example, that she could approach Caroline Drummond and start a simple conversation, for every subject that

Addie essayed, no matter how trivial, Caroline would seize and snap off like a brittle twig.

It was not so much that Caroline seemed to mind their being there, but she was so absorbed in her own plight — easily read after their first day there — of being a Philadelphia beauty caught in this cobwebby rural trap, that she wove her whole existence around the injury. She had made no comment beyond a long hard look when Addie and Rose-Anne had appeared at the supper table in their remade dresses, but the next day Addie had passed by the open door of her bedroom upstairs and had seen her sitting on the edge of the rumpled bed tearing at the collar of a fine blue watered silk dress. It was more than the practical seamstress in Addie could bear.

"Perhaps I could help you with that, Cousin Caroline," she suggested, pausing outside the door.

Caroline at once flung the dress from her. Her cheeks were flushed as she looked up at Addie.

"No, there's nothing to be done with it. It's all wrong. They aren't wearing that collar at all this year. I saw in my husband's New York paper. It's completely out of the fashion."

"It's very easy to change the collar on a dress," Addie pointed out. "What kind of collar would you fancy?"

"Why, it needs that shawl kind that comes down to here, and you fasten it with a brooch."

"Oh, I've seen those," Addie said cheerfully. "Only we need a very fine white lawn for it — "

"No, it wouldn't do. I don't want patchy things."

"It wouldn't look patchy; really it wouldn't. I've seen

84

dresses like that at the theater in Philadelphia, and I know just how to do it."

Caroline got up and drew her green velvet wrapper around her. She was suddenly bored, indifferent.

"It's no matter," she said. "My husband and I will be going to New York City one day soon and I will be able to shop for all the latest things." And she picked up the dress and handed it to Addie. "Here. Perhaps you or your little sister would like it."

Addie protested, but she took the dress and put it among her sewing things. Perhaps in a little time she would fix it and offer it back to Caroline. But she would have to make the offer carefully. For she could see in Caroline's dark eyes what it was that she resented. Not the fact that Addie had clever fingers and could restore a dress, but that Addie was of the city — that she knew all about city fashions and what ladies wore to the theater.

She got along well with Abel Drummond and he was unfailingly polite and cordial with her, but she was never able to ask him many questions, even about her grandfather, because he was always busy, coming or going. Jonah West was in and out of the house often too, sometimes taking a meal with them when he and Abel had matters to discuss in the evening. He lived in a small log house of his own a short distance up the road, she learned. She was still, after several days, mystified about what business occupied them so fully. This was, as far as she could tell, a farm. Yet neither of them did any farming; only Philip Hess did.

Rose-Anne, completely at home after the first day, knew more about it than she.

"It has to do with land," Rose-Anne told her privately. "Our grandfather owns enormous amounts of land hereabouts. And when he was well he had plans for it — I'm not sure about that part — but now that it appears he'll never be really well again, Cousin Abel and Mr. West are settling people on it. Trying to get shut of it, I guess. And there's a road being built; that takes much of their time."

It was a vague explanation with a great many parts missing, but it was more than Addie knew.

"Where'd you hear about it?" she asked suspiciously.

Rose-Anne blushed. "Cousin Philip told me."

Addie gave her a very direct look.

"He's not our cousin."

Rose-Anne looked at her shoes.

One thing Addie was looking forward to was the weekly visit of the doctor from the village. He had been coming each week for more than a year, Abel Drummond said, to examine Jeremiah Drummond.

"We'll ask him about your visiting your grandfather and helping with his care," Abel promised. "We could certainly use the help around here."

Addie clasped her hands together.

"Oh, I do hope he approves."

Dr. Patchett proved to be a small man with side whiskers and thin lips. Addie was not much impressed with his professional appearance. Even Bowen had made a better looking doctor than that, she thought privately. But she waited anxiously for him to come downstairs from the old man's room. When he did, his face had taken on angry color, and the whiskers seemed to be standing on end just as

Bowen's did when he was excited. He was shaking his head. Abel Drummond and Addie stood at the foot of the front stairs waiting for him.

"Mr. Drummond, will you please reason with your uncle before my next visit?" Dr. Patchett said irritably. "He needs to be bled . . . needs it badly, I'd say, and he refuses to let me near him. When I think of the poisons and dangerous humors that must be building up there, coursing through his body — "

Abel Drummond frowned wearily.

"I'll try to reason with him, Doctor. Meantime, his granddaughter — Oh, forgive me, this is Miss Adelina Trimble, our young cousin. Now do you think she could call on her grandfather? She and her sister are anxious to meet him and have even offered to take over some of the care of him."

Dr. Patchett looked at her, studying her with some wonder.

"Carlotta's girl?" he asked sharply. "But that was the whole trouble — that was what started all this — " He seemed to sense her bewilderment and made an attempt to settle his ruffled feathers. "Perhaps you haven't been told, my dear," he said more kindly. "But there was bad feeling when your mother ran off and married. Then when the old gentleman received word of her death — well, it struck him a terrible blow."

"I thought perhaps there was something like that," Addie murmured.

"We don't know what was in his mind, none of us," said the doctor. He lifted his shoulders. "But if he were to see you now it would surely stir up old sorrows, old griefs. I am sorry, Miss Trimble. I'm afraid I must counsel against it. He's a man very close to his Maker. Very close."

Addie said nothing but she felt depressed, dragged down. She had counted so much on the doctor's being in favor of it. And too, there was something that bothered her about Grandfather Drummond's being so close to his Maker, but not too close to put up a fight where Dr. Patchett was concerned.

She worked that afternoon under Rose-Anne's direction, turning out and cleaning the front parlor. It was not a job she cared for, but it gave her a chance to think. Rose-Anne was taking on the housecleaning a room at a time, planning the campaign like a general, and Addie mopped and polished as she was ordered, but all the time she worked she kept thinking and studying on the matter. And no matter how many times she argued it back and forth with herself, it always came out the same way. If you wanted to help someone and do for him, and if all you wanted was that person's welfare, then how could you possibly hurt him? Dr. Patchett might know all there was to know about bleeding and purging and that kind of business, but she guessed that perhaps he was not too smart in other ways. She made her decision right then about what she would do, but she said nothing of it even to Rose-Anne.

Next midday when the house was quiet and when the lank and lusterless Essie was sent upstairs with the invalid's tray, Addie was waiting at the top of the backstairs to waylay her.

"I'll take my grandfather his tray," she said in a sharp whisper. "Give it to me."

88

Essie peered at her in the dim hallway.

"I'm not allowed," she said sullenly.

"Oh, yes you are," Addie said with terse authority.

"I'm not. Old Upjohn'd whale me. Ain't anybody allowed except me and the family."

"Well, I'm family. And if you don't give it to me you'll get worse than a whaling. You'll be sent packing."

"What do you mean by that?"

"I'll tell Mrs. Upjohn about the eggs you've been stealing."

Essie swore at her quietly but she gave up the tray. Addie stood there for a moment in the shadowy hall, waiting for her to go back downstairs. Then quietly and carefully she pushed the door open.

He lay there in bed in a half-sitting position with pillows behind his head. His eyes were closed. Addie paused uncertainly and studied him for a moment. It looked to her as if he had been a big man and strong before his illness. Even now the look had not entirely left him. His head was large, his features sharp. He had thick gray hair that curled a little around his temples. One hand, the right one, lay on top of the covers, and it was a big square hand with long fingers. Underneath the covers his body looked thin and slight, but she judged that he must be very tall, even taller than Abel Drummond.

"Yes, come in," he said suddenly, and his eyes opened. They were deep blue — the same shade as Rose-Anne's, Addie thought with shock — but sunken now, the eyes of illness and age. He stared at her.

"Who are you?" he frowned.

Addie had rehearsed this part. She balanced the tray carefully and dropped a small curtsy, just as she had in *Lover's Letter.*

"I'm the new girl, sir," she said.

He went on staring for a time. Then he said without humor, "Are you any smarter than the old girl?"

Poor Essie, she thought. She's certainly getting the worst of it today.

"I couldn't say, sir," she answered, advancing with the tray.

He closed his eyes briefly, wearily, then opened them again and nodded toward a table by the bed.

"Put it there," he ordered. "Help me to sit up."

She did as she was told. The table, which was within reach of his right hand, was littered with papers, charts and drawings. She moved them a little to make room for the tray. Then she put an arm behind him and helped to raise him while she adjusted the pillows. She could feel the sharpness of his shoulder blades, but for all his thinness she still did not sense frailty there. There was a taut wiry feeling of muscle and sinew despite his spent appearance. As she adjusted the covers she noticed for the first time that his left hand moved with difficulty. In fact he moved it himself with the right hand as he made ready for the tray. There was a slight droop about the left side of his face too — not pronounced, but noticeable when he spoke. The corner of his mouth pulled down ever so slightly. Whatever his illness had been, it must have dealt him a powerful blow, for there was no mistaking what kind of man he must once have been. The strength, the authority, the capability, all could be seen faintly, but as shadows, no longer real. Only the sharp intelligence of the blue eyes looked as if it had survived undiminished. And even that was intermingled with weariness and a kind of acceptance of defeat. *A man of sorrows and acquainted with grief,* Addie thought, remembering the words from somewhere in the Bible.

She put the tray on his lap and stood back, thinking that perhaps she should leave at once. It might shame him if she watched him eat, in case he should be awkward or unsteady.

"Is there anything else I can do for you?" she asked.

He paid no attention to her question. He was frowning as he picked up his spoon. His mind was somewhere else.

"Are they still haying?" he inquired.

"I believe they are, yes, sir. They hope to finish today."

"Good," he murmured. "They'll have to start pulling flax then, before it toughens. Is it August yet?"

"It lacks a few days, I believe."

"Should be pulled before August. I must speak to Philip about it."

"Yes, sir."

"You tell him that, girl. Tell him to see me."

"I will, sir." It was apparent that old Mr. Drummond still worried about the farm, the crops, how everything was being managed. But he was querulous and sharp from his long illness. Had he perhaps become no more than a nuisance to all of them? Did Philip Hess only put up with him impatiently, listen to his orders and then slam out to do as he pleased? There was pain in the thought, and melancholy too. Just as there was melancholy in this room. A solitary cup with a spoon standing in it, hollowed-out

91

pillows, a book, a sheaf of papers within reach, and always, always, the lonely hours that filled the room with their heavy sluggish presence. Sick people became strangers to the world of up-and-doing, Addie reflected, and every relationship with them became an obligation. Old Mr. Drummond was smart enough to feel that. And when an illness was so long and so hopeless and when the only thing ahead was death —

Suddenly without caring whether it was the right thing to do, Addie pulled a small chair over near the bed and sat down, back straight, hands folded in her lap.

"You wouldn't mind if I sat with you for a minute, would you?" she asked.

His thick eyebrows shot up, again the left side lagging behind the right.

"Why would you want to do that?" he asked bluntly.

"I haven't anyone much to talk to around here," she said, stretching the truth only slightly.

"I don't care much for talk."

She changed the subject. "You seem to keep very busy," she observed, nodding toward the papers on the table.

"Just writing on air," he said bitterly.

"It looks like more than air."

"Well, 'tisn't. It's only a pastime."

"But what is it?" she persisted. "All those lines and squares — "

"You're mighty sassy!" he exploded. "None of your business!"

"I don't mean to be sassy," she said, not sounding too contrite. "I only wondered, is all."

He did not answer but went about the business of eating.

He ate sparingly, she noticed, and without much interest in the food. There was silence in the room for several minutes. Finally he dropped his spoon on the tray with a clatter and said, "It's a town."

Her eyes went to the papers again.

"What town?"

"A town that's never been built. Nor ever will be. Not by me anyway."

"Where would it be if you did build it?"

"Over to westward where there's a good stream. Two thousand acres there I've kept aside for it. I had in mind it could be the county seat."

He tossed it out casually, but it sounded to Addie like a huge undertaking. Her grandfather then had been a man of stature and influence.

"How would you ever go about doing that?" she asked, because all at once she really wanted to know.

"Building a town? Why, first you'd pick a good spot — that's what I've got there — and then you put up a mill. Now, you're so full of questions; riddle me this: What kind of mill would you put up first?"

The city girl floundered.

"What kind of mill?" she echoed helplessly.

"Yes. What kind? Grist mill? Saw mill?"

She thought for a moment. "Saw mill," she answered.

"More important to cut lumber than to grind flour?" he asked with a kind of sharp amusement.

"No, not more important exactly. But if it's a new place and there's no one settled there, there wouldn't be any grain to grind. Not the first year there wouldn't. But there'd be plenty of trees cut."

93

"Well, that's pretty good reasoning," he admitted. "Of course a place like my town could really use both, because it'd be near enough to farms so that they could haul the grain there and back. But people will settle near a mill, and there's the start of your town. Then your tradesmen come — tanner, smith, cooper. And pretty soon a tavern and a church and a school get built. And there you are."

Addie nodded to show she was following him. Then, "Must you always stay in that bed, sir?" she asked.

His features, which had shown some animation when he was talking of the town, grew stony and resentful.

"Why, no, only last night I went out dancing and tomorrow I plan to walk to Batavia."

Where there was malice, it seemed to Addie, there was still some life.

"All I meant was, couldn't you sometimes sit in that chair?" And she tipped her head toward a chair that stood near the window.

"Young lady, I dealt with that fool Patchett — well named indeed — already this week. Do I have to fight you off as well? The answer is no. I can't sit in that chair because I can't take the two steps it would take to get me there. Left leg doesn't work. And I can't use a cane because my left hand can't hold one."

"If I stood on your left side and you leaned on me, you could do it," she said. "And from that window you can see the flax fields. When they start cutting tomorrow you could watch."

"Pulling."

"What?"

"You don't cut flax. You pull it. Ruins the fiber if you cut it."

"You think about it," she said.

9

⁓⁓

THERE WAS an uproar in the kitchen late that afternoon. Caroline Drummond precipitated the thing, sweeping into the kitchen just as Mrs. Upjohn and Rose-Anne were embarking on preparations for supper, with Addie looking on. Mrs. Upjohn was explaining the making of biscuit dough while Rose-Anne watched.

"You got to cosy it along," Mrs. Upjohn said. "You handle it easy, never punch nor pound or it'll harden up on you. Now mind them bones!" she flung out worriedly to Essie, who was pulling apart a boiled chicken. And it was then that Caroline entered, her handsome face wearing a set look of nervous concentration.

"Mrs. Upjohn, where is the silver teapot?" she asked loudly, her anxious tone giving the matter importance.

Mrs. Upjohn stared at her, startled.

"Why, yonder in the dining room, Ma'am. It rests there on the shelf, doesn't it?"

Addie ducked into the storeroom to select two of last

fall's apples for the General and his friend. She returned through the wellshed connecting the summer kitchen with the main kitchen and paused to watch. Caroline had put on a dress today and she looked stylish and pretty. It was a soft lilac muslin that suited her well. Now she swished into the dining room and returned with the teapot. It was well shaped and costly looking, but black with disuse. She held it at arm's length.

"Just see there," she mourned. "I can't think how many months it's been since that was polished."

Rose-Anne was at once sympathetic.

"I noticed it myself, Cousin Caroline, when I was cleaning the dining room this morning. And I meant to get to it today, but the time slipped by me. It's a beautiful teapot."

"Boston silver," Caroline Drummond tossed off carelessly, giving the thing distinction by her very casualness. "And there's a creamer and sugar bowl and twelve spoons."

"Beautiful," Rose-Anne repeated.

"I can't think," Caroline went on in her clear sharp voice, "why we never have afternoon tea in this house."

Mrs. Upjohn wiped flour-coated arms on her large apron.

"Afternoon tea?" she echoed hollowly.

"Yes, certainly. In Philadelphia we had afternoon tea regularly."

"Well, it's just that having tea in the afternoon means pushing your supper later, and I don't think the men would like that. Mr. Drummond comes in hungry and so does Mr. West, if he's to eat with us, and Mr. Philip! He's so starved coming in from the fields he'd eat a hog on the hoof," Mrs. Upjohn finished with inelegant emphasis.

Caroline appeared to be only half-listening.

"Yes, well, I suppose in the country — Still, there's no reason why we shouldn't have it occasionally. And in any case, the teapot should certainly be kept polished. Essie! Help me bring these things from the dining room. We'll start at once polishing them. Here." She set the teapot down. "We can work at this end of the table."

Essie looked from Caroline to Mrs. Upjohn, enjoying the situation since she was, for once, blameless.

"I can do the chicken," Rose-Anne said.

Mrs. Upjohn nodded glumly, and Essie dropped the chicken into the bowl gleefully and wiped her hands on the hem of her skirt.

"We'll need rags," Caroline commanded, standing there regally and injecting total confusion into the preparations for supper which had been going along so smoothly.

Addie ducked out through the wellshed and headed with quick steps up the hill to the high pasture, thinking that afternoon tea with Caroline Drummond was a bleak prospect for the future.

General Strong was glad she had come, and he enjoyed the apple, but in his own rather proud way. His ancient companion was pathetically grateful and he stayed near Addie, nuzzling and wheezing, for several minutes. When she left them and came back down the slope she avoided the kitchen door, for she was sure the campaign was still being waged. Instead, she went around front and on out to the road. It was a glorious July afternoon. Shadows were beginning to lengthen a little, but there were still hours of daylight left. And probably, Addie surmised, hours before supper could be salvaged out of the upheaval in the kitchen.

She would take a short walk up the road in the direction she had not yet explored, away from the village.

The road was a pleasant one, overhung with branches and well traveled. Now at midsummer, the passing of wagons had already worn the ruts down fairly deep. Addie kept to the center where some grass grew and the walking was easier. Looking at the dust on her shoes, Addie realized that there had been no rain since they arrived at the farm. Still, it had made for good haying weather. She smiled to herself at how quickly she was picking up a country viewpoint. Also as she walked she puzzled on how to give Philip Hess the message from her grandfather about the flax. Outright? Just admit she had called on him? Or circumspectly, perhaps through Rose-Anne?

She had gone almost a mile before she rounded a bend in the road and came upon the log house. She knew at once that it must belong to Jonah West. It was a much more substantial house than Florinda's — there were two fine glass windows and a stone chimney — but it was very much a bachelor's house. There was no kitchen garden; there were no flowers except for the knotweed, chicory and wild pinks that scrambled and climbed everywhere. A shirt had been thrown over a scraggly sumac to dry. She knew that her grandfather had come here from New England, bought land, built it up, and finally had put up his good brick house, but before that he must have had a log house. That was the way it was done, she supposed. The glass windows and the stone chimney were touches he might have wanted, being the kind of man he was. Could this have been his house once? Now that she had seen him she could picture him here, could even picture his hands, large and square and capable, as they might have worked at notching the logs and laying them straight. Her mother would have been a small girl then. Little Carlotta. Had she played here in this dooryard? The thought took hold of Addie with all the power of years gone and irrecoverable, all the sadness for lost things. A memory was never truly lost, of course, while someone held onto it. A life remembered was still a presence felt. But one day Jeremiah Drummond would be gone and she and Rose-Anne would be back in Philadelphia and Abel and Caroline would leave, no doubt, for the city life Caroline loved, and there would be no one to remember, and this seemed almost too sad to be borne.

"Looking for something?" The voice made her lurch awkwardly, it startled her so. Jonah West must have come around the house from the back for he stood there now leaning against the corner and regarding her stolidly.

"I was just out for a walk," she answered. "Is this your house?"

" 'Tis for the moment. It belongs to the property."

His lounging stance, arms folded in front of him, prompted her to straighten her own shoulders.

"I don't wish to intrude," she said, keeping her voice pleasant but not liking him at all. Of all the people in the household he was the least clearly defined. Up to now she had harbored no opinion of him one way or the other. He seemed to move at Abel's direction, to come and go on business, to eat with them occasionally, and that was all. She thought him rather unkempt and his manners poor in comparison to Abel's. He was noisy at table. Yet he spoke almost nothing except roads, mail routes, plot divisions, and it was impossible to read his character. Up to now, that is.

At this moment it was quite clear that he resented her. It puzzled Addie but concerned her little, since he was not a person whose judgment she valued. And she was curious.

"Was this my grandfather's house once? Did he live here?"

He nodded but then offered nothing more.

"I thought as much." There was so much she still wanted to know, things she could inquire about if she could manage to close one eye to his bad manners. "Did you work for my grandfather before his illness?" she asked.

He seized the drying shirt from the sumac and wadded it up to bring into the house with him. In the doorway he paused and looked at her again, a slanting dark glance full of malice.

"Why don't you ask him all these things?"

"What do you mean by that?"

"You went to see him today, didn't you?"

"It wasn't any secret," she snapped back, wondering feverishly how he had found out. Essie, of course. It had to be Essie. "I intend to tell my cousin as soon as I see him." This was not quite true. She might have kept it to herself a little longer if Essie had not blabbed. "Besides, I don't see what it has to do with you."

The stocky shoulders came up again.

"Nothing. Nothing to do with me. I think it's fine. Why shouldn't you see if you can get something out of him before he dies? You should bring your little sister with her big blue eyes. That ought to turn the trick for sure."

Addie was horrified at this spite.

"I never even told him who I was!"

"But you will, I don't doubt. Sooner or later you will."

He disappeared into the house before she had a chance to answer again. It took her a moment to realize that she was standing there snubbed, and when she did she turned quickly and started striding back along the roadway. He was certainly a person of very poor character, she decided. From now on she would do her best to avoid any commerce whatever with Mr. Jonah West. It was only when she started up the green slope toward the big house that the thought struck her; was Jonah West one of the four thistles around Essie's pillow? And if so, had he won?

10

"I HOPE you won't be angry with me, Cousin Abel," Addie said that evening at the supper table. "I'm afraid I've done something against your wishes." She purposely kept her eyes away from Jonah West, who was taking supper with them in a clean but rather badly wrinkled homespun shirt.

Abel Drummond looked at her mildly.

"What's that, my dear?"

"I called on Grandfather today." She said it calmly, not making too much of it lest she appear to be giving it undue importance. She heard Rose-Anne's startled intake of breath. "I realize Dr. Patchett was against it," she went on. "I simply felt he was quite wrong. I know it was bold of me but I couldn't see how it could possibly hurt Grandfather. I didn't tell him who I was and I don't intend to — right away," she added, leaving a door open. "But I think he enjoyed my visit. Perhaps it even did him some good."

Abel Drummond looked at first distressed, then uncertain, and appeared to think it over. Suddenly he smiled.

"Good for you," he said decisively. "Why not indeed? I never did think old Patchett had more than his share of brains. And you're right, Addie. What harm can it possibly do him?"

Addie, who had been prepared for more of a to-do over it, felt relieved and a little triumphant. She went on eating, paying earnest attention to her plate, and only after a few minutes did she angle a swift side glance at Jonah West. He was not even looking at her, but was bent forward over his plate, fork held like a trowel.

This was the pleasantest meal they had sat down to since coming here. For the first time the dining room shone with polish and sparkle from Rose-Anne's scrubbing. Caroline's silver teapot gleamed on the shelf. Caroline herself appeared more relaxed and animated than usual, and even Philip Hess had managed to change into clean clothes and sit down with them. The chicken and biscuits had survived deliciously the tumult in the kitchen and in the center of the table was a glass bowl with Rose-Anne's raspberry preserves quivering moistly and catching the long sun rays like rubies.

For the first time too, it seemed to Addie, there was present some small feeling of family. A bond held them together, however tenuously, and reached out to include the sick man upstairs.

"I questioned him a little about what occupied his time," Addie went on. "He talked of the farm. And by the way, he wishes to speak to you about the flax, Philip. And then he told me about his town, the one he wished to build."

Abel nodded. "The dearest wish of his life."

"It seemed so to me as he spoke of it. He called it writing on air. He knows he can never carry it out now."

"No, that's true; he can't," Abel agreed. "But I'm doing everything I can to carry it out for him."

Addie looked at her cousin quickly. "*You're* building the town?"

"Just as he would want it, or so I hope."

"But he doesn't know! You should tell him; it would mean the world to him."

Abel sighed. "So I thought in the beginning. I went to him when he began to get back a little strength and tried to approach him about it very cautiously, to ask his advice and tell him my plans and so on. He became overwrought, overstimulated, feverish. It caused him a severe setback, so I said nothing more. Dr. Patchett was quite cross with me. The trouble was," and here Abel grinned, an engaging grin that made him look years younger, "Uncle Jeremiah wanted to boss the job run the whole thing — and it was too much for him. Natural enough though; he's been a man of affairs for years. Too much to expect him to take a back seat and watch others do his work."

Addie, remembering her grandfather's empty, hopeless look, thought that probably this was so. One more thing to remind him of the world outside, of which he was no part.

"But if he should improve?"

"Oh, my dear, what a day that would be for him! I think of it often, how I shall take him there — let him ride up and down the main street and see it all — the little houses, the garden plots, the mill and the smithy — "

There was a snort from across the table and all heads turned toward Jonah West, who had shoved his plate back

105

with a clatter and was now lounging back in his chair rudely. Abel looked at him with tolerance.

"There sits Thomas, the doubting one," he said good-naturedly, raising an admonishing finger. " 'Blessed are they that have not seen, and yet have believed,' " he quoted. "It's true, the houses and garden plots are not there yet, but they will be, they will. Our first concern is a road, and we are bending every effort toward that. The rest will come in good time. Our people are pitching in with a will to get the road through right now."

Rose-Anne had stopped eating and was listening too.

"What people?" she asked. "Where are they from?"

"Such people are from everywhere," Abel answered. "Human castoffs, the unwanted. But my particular little band is from Germany. Stout yeoman stock, all of them, wanting only a chance to live decently, build homes, become sturdy independent pioneers."

"They're city riffraff, that's what they are," Jonah West said loudly, and all eyes around the table went to him. He sucked at his teeth. "They don't know a plow from a plumb bob, any of 'em, and it would take some doing, even under the best of conditions, to make anything of 'em."

Abel looked down at the table and it seemed to Addie he was holding on to his temper.

"They were poor and luckless in their own country, yes. They were in danger of arrest for vagrancy and pauperism. I spoke for them through an agent in Hamburg, guaranteed their passage here, and now together we're building a town and a new life for them."

Addie glared at Jonah West and then asked Abel, "But

then they have no money to buy land from you; yet you spoke of their being free men."

"True, they have no money, but they have their hands. They'll pay with their work. No more than six years, as I figure it, with sharing crops and improving the land, and then it will be theirs free and clear. I'm figuring on three acres and a cabin for every family."

"Hah," said Jonah West.

Caroline Drummond spoke suddenly in her high clear voice.

"And when the town is built and everyone sees what my husband has done, he may even go into politics and become a big man in the state. We may go to live in Albany or one of the other cities."

Addie felt embarrassed for Abel Drummond, who had lowered his eyes and reddened at his wife's outburst. She could see that Caroline's excesses mortified him. She suspected his wish would be to stay here in this house and watch his town grow and prosper, to become a country squire and lead a quiet life.

The atmosphere around the table, which had been so warm and congenial, turned awkward. Addie floundered about, seeking a new subject.

"I had another adventure a few days ago," she said brightly. "I walked out past the back dooryard, up the hill and down across the meadow, and I came to a little log house with the oddest old woman living in it. And there was a boy living there too — almost a man, although it was hard to tell, for he seemed not right in the head — "

Caroline's hand gave a quick jerk that sent her water

glass over. Addie stopped talking and stared in astonishment at the spreading stain on the white tablecloth. Caroline was already on her feet, trembling and white-faced.

"What business is that of yours?" she shrilled. "Just because we've taken you in doesn't mean you have the right to go knocking and nosing at every door. My husband is the head of the house here. You should ask his permission before you start wandering about, snooping and prying!"

Addie was so shocked her mouth went suddenly dry and she struggled for words.

"I'm so sorry," she mumbled. "I'm really sorry, Cousin Caroline — "

But Caroline had already thrown down her napkin and swept out of the room.

"Oh, Cousin Abel, what have I done?" Addie pleaded unsteadily. She looked from one to the other around the table. Rose-Anne's face was white and scared, and Jonah West glowered at the tablecloth. Philip Hess went on eating, but with a dogged motion, and his face was a dark angry red.

Abel Drummond's mouth was thin and unhappy.

"It wasn't your fault, Addie," he said.

"Yes, yes, it was. Oh, I'm much too forward."

"No. My wife is extremely sensitive. And the truth of it is that the old woman, Florinda, frightens her. It's been a sore subject between us. Your grandfather let Florinda live on the property and there's nowhere else for her to go. I haven't the heart to throw her off, her and her boy. But she terrifies Caroline. She's a perfectly harmless old soul."

Perhaps, Addie thought, remembering the jars and cruets marked with poison symbols, remembering the fire that had started up in the cold fireplace with no touch of embers or spark. Or perhaps Caroline, with her fantasies and fears, saw more clearly than the others did.

"I wouldn't have upset her for the world," she said quite honestly. "I only meant to make conversation. I do hope she'll overlook it."

"She will, of course," Abel reassured her. "Please don't think any more about it."

But Addie did, and was silent, hardly touching the rest of the meal. She was heartsick at having spoiled their first congenial gathering as a family and, even more, regretted creating another uncomfortable situation for Abel Drummond.

He smiled at her across the wreckage of the table and said, "I'm afraid we're a rather strange household, my dear. This will pass, believe me."

Jonah West got up with an abrupt scrape of his chair, not excusing himself or even nodding to them, and left the dining room. Presently his voice and Caroline's could be heard coming from the front parlor. The tones were low and confidential and heightened Addie's dislike of Jonah; his behavior seemed exceedingly improper. But Abel showed no reaction whatever and went on to finish his meal. Presently Philip Hess rose and said in Rose-Anne's direction, "I'll bid you good evening, ladies."

Addie bade him a cool good evening back, but Rose-Anne managed a shy smile.

When they talked at bedtime in their own room,

Rose-Anne's mouth grew firm with disapproval and she looked as stern as it was possible for her to look.

"Addie, you have been bold," she chided.

"Oh, I know it," Addie agreed miserably. "I shouldn't have done any of those things, I suppose. But it didn't seem bad at the time. And as far as Grandfather's concerned, I'm still not sorry."

"Well, Cousin Abel didn't seem upset about that. Do you suppose I could visit him too?"

"I don't see why not. We'll let him get to know us and then one day we'll just tell him very gently who we are. But we'll make sure he's strong enough first."

"Oh, I would so like to. Is he very sick?"

"Yes, but — " Addie hesitated, not sure how to describe the feeling she had about her grandfather — that what he needed most was someone to believe he would be well again. "What do you think of Mr. Jonah West?" she asked, changing the subject.

"He's very untidy, isn't he? I don't think he bathes."

"But what do you think of his character?"

"I don't trust him. He seems a trashy sort to me."

"To me too. And another thing — "

"What?"

"Well, he seems to sort of — cater to Cousin Caroline."

"Yes, I've noticed. You don't suppose — "

"Remember that play, *The Faithless Wife*?"

"Oh, Addie, that was only a play."

"Even so."

"Well, don't let's think about that. Tell me about this funny old woman you met. Why do you suppose Caroline's so scared of her?"

"I can understand it in a way. She *was* odd."

"Were you scared?"

"I think I was a little bit."

It was quite a time before they both slept. And at that Addie slept less soundly than usual. There was noise from somewhere in the house. Banging and crashing and sounds of weeping. Caroline Drummond in her room with the brandy bottle. Presently Abel's voice could be heard above the clamor and it was sharp with anger. Patience worn threadbare, Addie thought unhappily. And all my fault.

11

CALAMITY, crisis and emotional outburst seemed to be taken in stride by the Drummond household, however. By the time Addie and Rose-Anne came downstairs to breakfast the next morning, everyone but Caroline was up and about. A new day's work was under way and not a word was mentioned about the night before. Nor did it appear to be consciously avoided; it seemed entirely forgotten.

Abel Drummond called a hello to them but remained in the dining room with Jonah West, going over a great sheaf of papers. They seemed to be reckoning up accounts of some sort. The kitchen was at sixes and sevens, for Philip Hess had brought in a bucket of clay and was patching the inside of the fireplace oven.

"A great crack right there in the lining of it," Mrs. Upjohn pointed out to the girls. "Of course patching's a job to save for winter or bad weather usually, but as I said to Philip, it makes me nervous and skittery thinking I can't use that oven if I should want to, and there's no better time than now when we got the summer kitchen to fall back on. It beats me what put that crack in it anyhow."

Addie showed a perfunctory interest and then went to help herself to tea and toasted bread. Rose-Anne appeared to be fascinated, however. She peered inside the opening to examine the crack and asked Philip a number of questions about the consistency of the clay.

"I thought I'd get at it early," he explained to her, "for we're going to start on the flax field today. There's work aplenty there. You have to manage flax just so or you'll spoil it."

"Could I help?" Rose-Anne asked unexpectedly, and Addie looked at her in alarm. Now that she had turned the house inside out to clean it, was Rose-Anne going to start working in the fields? Philip blushed.

"It's hard work," he said, looking at her.

"I don't mind work."

"No, it's too hot in that field for you. But you could come and watch a little if you want to. Later it has to be retted and then broken on the crackle. Maybe some of that you could help with."

"All right." Rose-Anne hesitated. "What does all that mean?"

"Well, retted — that means rotted, really. You have to soak it in water to loosen the fiber and then you dry it. And then when it's dry you break it on the flax brake — the crackle, we call it. It's a big bar that you slam down across the flax."

"Oh, I'd like to help with that."

"All right." He stared at her for a minute longer and

moist clay dropped off his hands onto Mrs. Upjohn's clean floor. Addie looked at it.

"Could I have a handful of that?" she asked.

He pulled his eyes away from Rose-Anne.

"What, this? Why, surely; take what you want."

Addie finished her tea hurriedly and went over to scoop a small lump of clay out of the bucket. She formed it into a ball, patting and kneading it, and then she wrapped it in a cloth and stuck it in her pocket. I have some patching of my own to do, she thought.

She waited until the job in the kitchen was finished and Philip had left. Shortly after, Rose-Anne went out and strolled in the direction of the flax field. Abel and Jonah were still in the dining room; she could hear their voices. She went quietly up the backstairs to her grandfather's room. She no longer had anything to hide, but silence was likely to be the path of wisdom around here, she was learning.

Old Jeremiah's eyes came at once to the door as she pushed it open, and some little spark in them made her feel pleasure laced with a touch of triumph. She was sure he had been watching for her. She dropped him a curtsy and bade him a good morning, but then wasted no more time on preliminaries, but went straight to the big chair by the window and arranged it so that a person sitting in it would have a good view of the blue-flowered flax field. A warm woolen shawl was folded across it, and she placed this so that it could be dropped around his shoulders. She did it all with quick decisive motions, as if to forestall argument, and then she turned to him and said, "There, now. I'll stand on

114

your left side. Put your arm across my shoulders and don't be afraid to let me support your weight if you feel unsure of yourself. I'm very strong."

He seemed to study her face, but only for seconds, as if to determine whether he could trust her, and she guessed that any number of thoughts were working in his head. Fear that he might fail in even this simple exercise, mistrust of a brash servant girl who made out to know more than the doctor, hopelessness because, after all, what good would it all do — but more than any of these, determination to try.

"Don't expect to see me dance a fandango," he growled.

"I don't," she said calmly. And then, because this would be the hard part, this space of seconds, she took a chatty tone and plunged into conversation as his arm came across her shoulders and she felt his heavy weight. "Philip's already working at the flax," she said, pulling him up from a sitting position, his long nightgown strained over thin legs. "He wanted to be out and at it early, but he had to stop and mend a crack in Mrs. Upjohn's kitchen oven first. She said it really should have waited for a rainy day but it made her nervous, having her oven not in working order, and I guess you know how Mrs. Upjohn is when her mind's set to something." Straining and panting, he had covered the two steps to the chair. Sweat stood out on his forehead. Addie eased him down into the chair gently and folded the shawl about his shoulders. From the foot of the bed she brought a quilt to cover his legs.

"There, now," she said, and she struggled to keep her voice offhand because unexpectedly she felt like crying. "There, now. That wasn't any great to-do, was it?"

He looked about him in an unbelieving way — at the

room seen from this new angle, at the chair, at her, and then through the window at the fields. For some time he did not answer her and she wondered if he was having trouble with his emotions too. And then at last he said, "That flax looks like a fair crop to me."

He sat in the chair for a quarter of an hour and the time was so filled with questions that Addie felt dizzy with all the answers she was expected to give, many of which she did not know. Had Philip kept on any of the extra hands once the haying was done? How was the corn doing? It would soon be time to look to that. Was Philip satisfied with the wheat? What about the kitchen garden — the vegetables and herbs — was anybody minding it? Woman's responsibility, but who there was to tend it in this house, he couldn't say, and it was important to have those vegetables and some boneset and tansy drying for winter complaints. Would she look to it and give him an accounting? And who was that girl with Philip? Another new hired girl? Well, there was certainly work enough around here.

Addie did her best to keep up with him and then finally insisted on helping him back into bed. He protested, but she could see he was weary.

"I'll come again soon," she said. She reached into her apron pocket and pulled out the clay. "In the meantime, here's something you can be doing. Take it in your left hand."

He frowned, but he let her press the damp clay into his helpless hand.

"I don't know exactly what it is made your hand and leg give out that way," she said. "But I do know they won't get strong again without exercise. And the first thing to work

116

on is the hand, because as soon as it's a little stronger, you can hold a walking stick in it, and then you can start exercising your leg. Keep this handy and work it around and squeeze it as often as you can." She was fairly sure of her ground here, because she had seen Mancuso, the great wire walker, take a bad tumble and land on his wrist. He had worked all one winter at the clay exercise to strengthen his ailing hand. "And while you're working on that, I'll massage your legs every day and help you to limber them up." This was a somewhat bolder suggestion, and she thought he might be angry at it, but she had seen dancers needing this treatment and she knew how it was done.

He thought about it for a moment and then said slowly, "Well, perhaps. I don't know as it'll do any good."

"I'll be back," she promised.

When Rose-Anne came in, warm and damp but excited from her morning in the flax field, Addie asked her, "Where's the kitchen garden?"

"Right back of the house."

Addie lowered her voice. "I visited with Grandfather again this morning. He's worried about it. It's vegetables and herbs. The woman of the house is supposed to tend it, but you know."

Rose-Anne nodded and they both considered Caroline Drummond.

"Then it's certainly not getting tended. I mean, Philip has much too much to do. I'm sure he hasn't time."

"Well, perhaps we could do it. Ask Philip what it needs. I guess maybe we have to pull weeds or some such thing."

"Oh, I will. I'll ask him." Rose-Anne's face lighted up.

117

Better than all the mopping and scrubbing they had been doing, Addie reasoned. At least it would be work in the open air and good exercise in the bargain. She didn't see that there was anything so tricky or mysterious about this business of farming. Once you got the hang of it, that is.

Philip showed them the kitchen garden that afternoon, a flourishing but weedy plot just a short distance behind the house. He had put it in himself in the spring, hoping to keep it up, but he had not found the time. What it needed was a good hoeing, and the weeds pulled between the rows, soil loosened around the plants and so on. Turnips, carrots, squash. Addie sized it up and said it didn't seem any great chore to her.

That night when she went to bed there was a knifelike pain between her shoulder blades and a sunburn that stung her face and the back of her neck. Rose-Anne seemed quite unbothered.

"Wasn't it wonderful, Addie? Seeing it all come into rows and the plants with room to breathe again? Tomorrow we should carry some water out there for them."

Addie groaned at what she had set in motion.

12

It was in such small ways that their days took shape and the girls found themselves fitting into life on the Drummond farm. It was an even, repetitious pattern and one they were scarcely aware of. It was the shuttle on the loom, riding in and out to form a design best seen at a slight distance.

Now there was never a day that Addie or Rose-Anne did not spend some time with old Jeremiah Drummond, helping him to his chair, exercising his thin legs. He accepted Rose-Anne's presence without question, and she was particularly good at keeping him informed with news of the farm, since she knew more about it than Addie. She asked his advice on the tending of the kitchen garden and reported any small successes in its care. She brought a ripening bean pod for his examination and he pronounced it none too poorly for all its early neglect. He seemed pleased that someone was taking over the duties that rightly belonged to the farm wife, and Addie began to realize the complexity and importance of such a person. Caroline Drummond's aristocratic presence must be a constant source of irritation to him, she thought.

Under this daily regimen it became apparent that old Jeremiah was improving and gaining strength. The gains were slight but they were steady, and it pleased Addie to think that soon, perhaps before summer's end, he might be able to take a few cautious steps with the aid of a walking stick. When that happened she knew that it would be only a matter of time before he could go in the carriage with Abel to see the progress on the town, and this was the thing she longed for above all else.

She thought it best not to say too much of this to Abel Drummond until success was a little nearer and more assured, but she did not try to keep it secret either. One day she mentioned in an offhand way that she was encouraging the old man to exercise.

"Do you think that's wise?" Abel asked anxiously. "Dr. Patchett certainly wouldn't approve."

"But it seems to agree with him."

"To inexperienced eyes it may seem to, yes. But Patchett has warned of overexcitement of the blood. Perhaps it's only building his hopes beyond all reason. I feel it would be wiser to leave things as they are."

Addie stared at him, a little deflated. She had not dreamed Abel would object to anything that was directed toward helping the old man, but the concern in his voice was certainly genuine. Then almost at once her natural buoyancy took over and reassured her. There were some people who never dared tempt fate with good fortune, who felt that to be overly optimistic only offended providence and brought on ill luck. Abel was such a one, she feared; he was worried lest any sign of improvement in old Jeremiah might prove false and be the harbinger of more trouble to come. People like that were best kept in the dark until you could show them results.

"Whatever you wish, Cousin Abel," Addie said agreeably, but she kept her own inward reservations.

"Good girl," he said, and looked relieved. Then he added, "Have you told him yet?"

"Told him?"

"Who you are."

Addie looked down. "No," she said. "Perhaps later."

And this was hard to explain to Abel, or indeed to herself. She wanted to let her grandfather know who she was and disagreed completely with Dr. Patchett that it would hurt him in any way. There was a surprising amount of strength in him, she thought. But still she hesitated, and admitted to herself that it was not fear for him that held her back, but for herself. Now he accepted her and Rose-Anne and let them help him. But the past was still a riddle to her. Old grudges, old resentments might lie there. Dr. Patchett had hinted that their mother's death had brought on this illness. If that were true, would he welcome them warmly as his granddaughters or would he hate them as reminders and heirs of an unhappy memory?

In any case she felt, although she was not patient by nature, that in this case patience was the best course. *There's a divinity that shapes our ends, rough-hew them how we will,* she thought, remembering *Hamlet* once more. She would wait for the Divinity to work, to give her some sign when the time was right.

121

Then after a long spell of dry hot weather came an interlude of rain. And no soft summer rain either, but a cold windy rain that brought out shawls and made Mrs. Upjohn light a fire on the kitchen hearth and go about slamming the shutters of the pleasant summer kitchen. Caroline Drummond, after her outburst of that one night, had resumed her stance of aloofness and indifference. She kept to her room, demanding a footstove and periodic trays of hot tea which Addie or Rose-Anne brought to her. She had a fresh supply of newspapers and several new novels and she was occupied by the hour poring over them. Her absence made the kitchen a cosier, pleasanter place, and Addie did not resent the rain at all. It relieved her of the eternal weeding and hoeing in the kitchen garden, and there was something friendly and protected, a happy, closed-in feeling that she enjoyed. Even the striped barn cat, who never bothered with the house or its inhabitants in good weather, crept in and curled snugly by the fire, tail wrapped around its feet, its purring a backdrop for the other kitchen sounds.

It was, except for old Jeremiah, a house full of women. Philip Hess was always busy. Now with the wet weather he mended harness and tools in the barn. Jonah West had been gone for several days, taking care of matters at the new settlement of Drummondtown. Abel had gone off in a different direction, and Addie knew that his errands were of a more delicate and important nature, for she had now learned that he visited important men in the state, wealthy businessmen, politicians, landowners. A scheme like this — building a whole new town, putting in a road — was an expensive one, and even though a man might be rich in land as her grandfather seemed to be, still there was a constant need for money. Tools had to be obtained for farming, road-building and house-raising; cattle were needed to provide labor and food, sheep to start flocks; hogs were always an indispensable item in a new settlement. Men who had the means to help had to be approached, and she supposed that Abel with his soft reasonable speech, his dreams of the new town, was a convincing speaker on the subject. It kept him traveling a great deal and they saw him now only every few days. Still, Addie could not say that she minded it. With Caroline keeping to herself most of the time, they were a happy congenial group when they gathered in the kitchen. Even Philip, when he joined them at odd intervals, was pleasant and managed to smile occasionally. Rose-Anne had accomplished that, of course, by the simple expedient of managing to have him fall in love with her. It had happened before and Addie took it as of no great account; for the moment it made things friendlier.

Now, with the rain streaming down and the wind setting up a howl in the chimney, Addie sat with a bit of mending in her hand and let the warm sounds and smells of the kitchen fold around her like a tucked-in quilt on a winter night. Near the hearth Essie sat with a bowl of peas, but she snoozed as much as she shelled. Rose-Anne stood at Mrs. Upjohn's elbow, watching every step of the way to learn the business of muffin-making. One pan was already in the oven, sugar-topped and blueberry-crammed, and the fragrance in the kitchen was so heady that Addie kept taking deep breaths and idling over her stitches.

"There, now," Mrs. Upjohn said. "We'll just slide those in and whilst we wait for 'em, why don't you two little ladies give me a verse or a story for entertainment, something from the stage, like." Mrs. Upjohn had a great fondness for this sort of thing, and when the kitchen was not too busy, they would regale her with pieces they had memorized or heard others perform. "That one you started yesterday — about the spy — now how did that turn out?"

"Oh, *The Glory of Columbia*," Addie said. "All right. Well, you remember how they caught the spy André, and although there were attempts to save his life, he was hanged."

"I know. I remember," Mrs. Upjohn said earnestly. "Strung him up, didn't they?"

"They did." This play, one by the great playwright William Dunlap, was fresh in the girls' minds since they had just taken part in it on July fourth. "All right, the final scene is at Yorktown, and there's scenery to show the town and the British lines, and then you hear cannonading from the batteries — "

"You really hear that?" Mrs. Upjohn's eyes were wide.

"Oh, to be sure. Fearful loud too. And then Washington and other officers come in — "

"You be Washington," Rose-Anne said. "You know the lines better. I'll be the chorus."

Addie put down her mending and got up, striking a commanding pose.

"Thanks, my brave countrymen! Our toils are past. It now requires not the spirit of prophecy to see, we have gain'd our country's independence. May that spirit — something something I forget in here — remain pure and unimpaired, for then long will she be free and happy."

"The fight is done! The battle won! Our praise is due to

124

him alone, who from his bright eternal throne, the fates of battles and of men decides!"

Rose-Anne, the chorus, was flushed with excitement as she delivered her lines.

"And after that," Addie explained, "a transparency comes down right above Washington's head."

"Lord save us! What's that?"

"A thin curtain," Addie explained. "And there's an eagle on it carrying a laurel crown and it's held right over Washington."

"All hail to Columbia's son!" Rose-Anne shouted. "Immortal Washington! By fame renown'd, by victory crown'd — " She broke off with a startled look as a loud pounding came at the kitchen door. The three of them, performers and audience, stared at each other and then looked toward the door.

"Oh, shoot now," Mrs. Upjohn said with irritation. "I wanted to hear the end of it. Just hold on a minute." She lumbered heavily toward the back door. "Who's out in a storm like this anyway?" she grumbled, and flung the door open.

Two figures stood there, a man and a woman, both of them drenched, the woman sagging so wearily that the man's arm around her seemed to be all that was holding her up. Mrs. Upjohn stared for a startled instant, then stepped back to let them in.

"What is it?" she demanded. "What brings you here? No, come in, come in. You can tell us later. But such a day! Such a storm! Why ever would you be out in it? Here, my dear, here by the fire."

She led the woman over to a stool by the hearth opposite

the one where Essie sat, now erect and wide-eyed with interest. Addie and Rose-Anne stared as Mrs. Upjohn lifted the sodden cape from the woman's shoulders, and both girls gave startled gasps and glanced at each other. Mrs. Upjohn stood as if frozen. Then, coming to briskly, she draped the cloak over a low bench close to the heat to dry out. She turned and looked at the man severely.

"You came on foot?"

He nodded.

"From the town? From Drummondtown?"

Again the nod.

Mrs. Upjohn shook her head.

"Thought you weren't from hereabouts. Well, it's a mercy she didn't have that baby on the way in some haystack or other."

The man — he was very young, Addie noticed, hardly more than a boy — lifted a hand to his forehead, and something in the gesture made Addie's heart go out to him. It was such a lost, weary motion, as if every ounce of his strength had been used up.

"Here you, get up from there," Mrs. Upjohn ordered, aiming a random kick at Essie. "Now. Sit there, up to the fire," she told the young man. "Let that heat get to you. I'll make you both something hot to drink. I daresay you could use some food too."

The young man shook his head.

"I am all right," he said, picking his words with difficulty. His speech was heavily accented. "*Aber meine Frau —* " He hesitated and started over. "My wife — *sie ist kranke* — sick — " He floundered, quite lost.

Mrs. Upjohn had already swung the kettle on its crane

over the hot part of the fire. Now she leaned over the woman. No, not a woman, Addie observed, watching. A young girl. No older than she. Maybe no older than Rose-Anne. The girl's face was drawn and sallow and her thin light hair, loose from its binding, hung wet and limp on her shoulders. Drops of water dripped from it onto her dress.

"She's not fevered," Mrs. Upjohn said, putting a hand to the girl's forehead. "I don't know but what she's just wore out. You just set there, dear, and get your strength back."

The girl's eyes lifted to Mrs. Upjohn's face briefly.

"*Danke,*" she whispered.

Mrs. Upjohn glanced back at Addie and Rose-Anne.

"She's thanking you," Addie said.

"They're German folk," Mrs. Upjohn said, "from the new town. Do you know their tongue?"

"Only a few words," Addie said. The summer before they had toured Pennsylvania with the company and many of the settlers in that area were Germans. Bowen had even featured a translation of *Richard III*, greatly condensed, and called it *Der Falsche König.*

"Maybe once they've had something hot, we can make out what it is they want," Mrs. Upjohn said. "You girl," she ordered Essie, "go fetch that ham from the storeroom, and a loaf of bread. Bring a cheese too. Dearie," she addressed Rose-Anne, "you mind those muffins or I might forget and burn 'em. I think some hot milk would do this girl good. Now you, mister, you'd like something stronger, I don't doubt. Addie, right over yonder behind the egg crock you'll find a bottle of spirits. I keep it for such occasions."

Within seconds the young girl's hands were curved

around a mug of hot milk with a sprinkle of nutmeg over its top. The young man was drinking a steaming toddy and, while Rose-Anne kept watch over the browning muffins, Mrs. Upjohn was setting about right and left with her big kitchen knife, slicing off thick pink slices of ham, crusty brown bread fresh from the morning's baking, and wedges of cheese that fell away in moist chunks.

She filled a heaping plate for the young man and handed it to him, but he did not touch the food, only looked worriedly at his wife, who seemed too weary and dispirited to show any interest in the plate Addie held out to her. Addie knelt down beside her and broke the cheese into small pieces.

"Here, now," she said gently. "You'll like this. Mrs. Upjohn made it herself, and she's first-rate. Try a little. *Essen Sie, bitte.*"

The girl glanced shyly at her and whispered again, *"Danke."* Timidly she took a small piece of cheese and ate it and, with Addie coaxing and helping and making use of the small handful of German words she could remember, she began to eat the rest of the food. When he saw her eating, her husband started on his. In minutes both plates were empty.

Addie exchanged a knowing look with Mrs. Upjohn.

The young man addressed a few words in German to his wife then, and she answered briefly and seemed to be trying to summon up a weak smile.

"We thank you," he said slowly. "Most kind." He was still clumsy with his words, but with the help of food and warmth he seemed able to express himself better.

"We had not such weather when we started out," he said.

128

"The storm caught us along the way. We had to take shelter."

"But why ever did you come all that way?" Mrs. Upjohn asked.

"We would like to see Mr. West," the young man said, only he called it "Vest."

"Mr. West isn't here," Mrs. Upjohn said. "I don't know but what he'll be back soon, though."

"We thought Mr. West was at Drummondtown," Addie said frowning.

The young man shook his head.

"It's long we have not seen him, and I must talk to him."

"Is there — some trouble?" Addie inquired.

The young man's face darkened, but he did not answer. Presently, taking in their curious expressions, he said with some dignity, "Excuse me. I did not say my name. I am Otto Langen and this is my wife."

Addie and Rose-Anne both curtsyed and introduced themselves and Mrs. Upjohn. The young wife was looking at them with shy glances which darted from one to the other. Addie felt self-conscious at their own appearance; although they were dressed in their hand-me-down clothes and old shawls, still they looked clean and neat, their hair was brushed and tied back, and they were both rosy with sun from their garden chores. Also, there was the plenty and lavish goodness of the kitchen around them — the fruity fragrance of the muffins which Rose-Anne was taking from the fireplace oven, the mounded eggs, the plump loaves. Somehow those two empty plates and the young wife's pale weary look told her that where the Langens came from there was less than enough to eat.

"Well, then," Mrs. Upjohn said decisively, "that gets us all acquainted. And I wouldn't doubt but what we'll see Mr. West and Mr. Abel Drummond too before nightfall, for I'm certain this was the day they set for coming back." She glanced at the trays Rose-Anne was placing on the table. "Why don't we all have us a muffin whilst we're waiting?"

13

It was late in the day when Jonah West arrived. He pushed through the kitchen door sodden and glowering and his eyes, when he saw the Langens, narrowed to dark slits.

"Otto! What are you doing here?"

The young man stood, looking anxious.

"Mr. West — I must see you. Very important."

"You and your woman walked all this way?" Jonah West was not pleased, Addie could tell.

"We are all right. We have been fed, most kindly."

West dropped a leather saddlebag on the floor and went over near the fire between Otto Langen and his wife.

"Well, what is it?" West's glance flickered over Addie and Rose-Anne.

"Mr. West, we are worried about the winter," the young man began hesitantly. *"Wir haben keine —"* He paused, struggling for the right words in English.

"Winter!" Jonah West exploded. "It's barely August. Winter's months away."

131

"*Ja*, I know, but — "

West spoke to him in German then, not easily, but in choppy phrases which Addie could not understand. His German was poor, she could tell. Probably he had picked it up from the band of settlers at the town site. Otto Langen answered him first in German, then in halting English. The conversation became heated and the two languages intermingled, interrupted each other. Addie caught phrases here and there.

"Twenty bullocks — that should be — *schlachten*, what does that mean? They did? Why didn't you stop them? Those were supposed to fatten during the summer and then — But how did they — "

And Otto Langen, excited and gesturing, "I tried! They do not listen, and now fourteen are gone!"

"Fourteen!" Jonah West swore thumpingly and Addie saw Rose Anne cringe slightly. "But they don't know how! And salt — *Salz* — "

It was a bewildering exchange which Addie could not make head or tail of, but there was no mistaking the fury in Jonah West's voice. Then finally Otto Langen drew a deep breath and said, "I came to tell you — we go to the Friends. My wife and I. For the winter. We will work for our keep and they will help when the baby comes. At Seneca Lake there are the Quakers. They will take us in."

Jonah West glowered. "If you go, others will go."

"I cannot help that. I must take care of my wife."

"Oh, go to hell and go to the Quakers!" Jonah shouted. "Good riddance to the lot of you!" And he stamped angrily from the room, his wet boots leaving tracks on the floor.

The young man drew himself up with some dignity,

although his face was flushed. His wife was trembling at the sounds of violence. Addie went over to her and put a hand on her shoulder.

"We go on our way now," Otto Langen said.

"Oh, fiddle, no such a thing," Mrs. Upjohn retorted. "Just keep your seats by the fire. You're not takin' that girl anywhere until she's had a chance to rest up and the storm's passed. We'll spread a straw tick on the floor in the summer kitchen and when Mr. Abel Drummond comes home he'll know what to do. He's the head of the house around here," she said firmly, relegating Jonah West to his proper position.

"Why, we must help them, of course." Abel Drummond's voice was calm and reasonable and now the kitchen, which had seemed a battleground, was a place of quiet and sanity. It had been close to dark when he arrived home through the storm, and his face had been weary from travel. Yet he had turned all his attention at once to the Langens and had listened to Otto's story with patience and concentration.

Mrs. Upjohn had made no attempt to set a proper table in the dining room, but simply kept bringing out food — slicing, ladling and filling plates. Wet boots were thrown in corners, wet outer garments were drying on pegs and chairs. Essie washed and dried dishes sullenly at a large wooden tub in the corner, and candles were brought as the night of storm and darkness closed in. Addie, hurrying in and out of the cool room with Rose-Anne, kept her ears open.

"Are many talking of going to the Quakers?" Abel asked.

"Many, yes."

Abel turned to Jonah West. "Now we can't have that, Jonah. You know it as well as I. There won't be a town without people in it. Of course we must help them through the winter."

"How?" Jonah West shouted. "Do you know what I had to pay for those twenty oxen? Two hundred pounds! And now they've slaughtered fourteen of 'em. In summer! I told them they should let them fatten on grass and wait for winter — "

"Well, it's done," Abel said with some sadness. "A wrong thing, a mistake, but done. And perhaps the meat won't be a total loss."

"Of course it will," Jonah growled. "They haven't enough salt; I know that for a fact. And all they've got are some log troughs which won't be large enough, and I'm sure they leak in the bargain. I'll start out at first light and see what I can do, but after this rain it'll turn hot again, I don't doubt. There'll be no saving it. It'll be full of maggots and smelling to heaven."

Abel shook his head sadly.

"All right, it's a mistake, Jonah. And maybe there'll be more mistakes. But we've got to do what we can. We've got to see that these people are fed through the winter."

"How?" Jonah demanded again. "We can't pick food out of the air."

"We'll borrow from Trapper Egan and Colonel Burke and we'll see if we can bargain for some more oxen. There are still six left — "

"How can we borrow? We owe already."

"I'm sure Egan will extend credit. Burke too. They know it's good investment."

"I say let 'em go to the Quakers and take our chances on starting things up again in the spring. All you'll have will be thirty-nine hungry mouths the whole winter. Thirty-nine people idling the time away — nothing accomplished — "

"If they leave, they'll never come back. It'll be the end of the town. Jonah, I won't be crossed in this." Abel's face grew angry and his voice rose. He strode back and forth across the kitchen. "You're to do as I say. And for once — no argument. Is that understood?"

Jonah let his breath out with a huffing sound of exasperation and strode from the room. Otto Langen looked anxiously toward Abel as though trying to read there how much he could depend on this new resolve and just what the words between the two men signified. Abel lowered his voice and seemed to bring himself back under control by deliberate effort.

"Please don't worry, Otto," he reassured the young man. "We will see to it that you're taken care of through the winter. It's going to be fine. Now you must rest here with us and wait for the storm to pass. I think it's blowing over now. And tomorrow we will send you back in a wagon. It can be returned later. Your wife should not walk such a far distance."

He placed a hand on the young man's arm as he left the room, but Addie could see the deep lines of trouble on his face.

The two girls waited until they were alone in their room and preparing for bed before talking about the incident, as they had grown accustomed to doing. Rose-Anne, ordinarily as gentle as a May lamb, was the first to explode.

135

"Addie, if I were a man and had the strength, I'd like to take that Mr. West by the hair of the head — "

"I don't blame Cousin Abel for losing his temper with him. I'd have lost mine long ago in his place."

"Mr. West seems to have no feeling whatever for those poor people."

Addie nodded. "I was thinking about other things too." She paused and Rose-Anne gave her a direct look.

"About him being in charge there at the new town?"

"I suppose it isn't fair to say, for we don't really know. But you heard them talk. About being in debt, about borrowing. And we know how hard Cousin Abel's been working to get important men around the state to invest in Drummondtown. He hasn't the time to be there himself and see how things are going. He leaves it all in Mr. West's hands, and what if — "

"What if he's stealing, you mean," Rose-Anne said slowly.

Addie sat down on the edge of the bed and looked up at her sister. "Well, he could be."

"Of course it wasn't his fault about the cattle being slaughtered."

"Indirectly it was. I mean, he was supposed to be there looking after things and he wasn't. We know the Germans are city people. Cousin Abel told us that. They don't know country ways and they've got to be instructed in such matters."

"But how could he steal, exactly?"

"He mentioned a price, didn't he? Two hundred pounds. I don't know anything about prices for cattle, but two hundred pounds is a fearful sum. Suppose he wasn't charged two hundred pounds for them at all. Suppose he was charged only something like one hundred and put the rest in his own pocket."

"Oh, Addie!"

"It would certainly account for why he was so riled about the fourteen that were killed. If he had to buy more, it might come out about the price being false in the first place."

Rose-Anne pulled the ribbon she was wearing and let her hair fall around her shoulders.

"And there isn't a thing we can do, is there?"

"No." Addie began unbuttoning her dress with jerky haste. "I just wish I could get over there and see that town myself. I bet I could tell."

"But it's far. A good day's walk. It took the Langens nearly two, although that was on account of her, I suppose."

"I feel so bad for Cousin Abel. And even worse for Grandfather."

Rose-Anne undressed quietly and slipped into her long nightgown. Addie did the same and they both knelt by the bed to say their prayers. Outside the storm was letting up, the pounding of the rain growing thinner and softer. Rose-Anne closed her eyes, then opened them again as though something still troubled her.

"I certainly don't care much for Mr. West's language either," she said, pursing her pink lips.

Addie interlaced her fingers and put her elbows on the bed.

"That's the least of our worries," she grumbled.

They were both awake and downstairs early to see the Langens off in the stout farm wagon Abel had provided.

137

The rain had passed and the sky was a clear washed blue.

"Drive easy," Mrs. Upjohn was counseling, piling hams, jugs, loaves and quilts into the wagon with the bewildered girl. "Let the horse take his time. There'll be mud, you know, and you don't want to mire down."

Addie went up to the side of the wagon and reached out a hand to the young wife.

"*Auf Wiedersehen,*" she said, and was surprised to feel the pressure of the girl's hand squeezing hers. She struggled to remember more words, but could not get them together. "Please send for me if you need me," she said, speaking clearly to try to make her understand. "Please let me be your friend." Then she remembered something. "What is your name? *Wie — Wie heissen Sie?*" she asked awkwardly.

"Elsa," the girl said in a low voice.

14

THE DAYS wore away, dropped one after another like ripe fruit from a tree. Summer, which had once stretched ahead endlessly, a long and dusty road, had grown suddenly foreshortened. Crickets sounded now in the soft evening, reminding them all of mortality, cautioning against the swollen satisfaction which summer's fullness brought. Winter's coming, winter's coming, they shrilled.

In the city, Addie recalled, summer had meant different things. More fruits and vegetables, for farm vendors came in early in the morning and cried their wares on street corners. And there was dust under one's feet, and thirsty horses bending to the troughs at the curbside. There were bellyaches now and then, and she recalled her mother growing indignant and blaming tainted meat. Once in a while Mrs. Brindley at the boarding house had had brisk quarrels with the milk seller, claiming the milk had turned.

Here on the farm summer was a different thing. The long days that lasted into evening, the dust, the heat, were only trappings, unimportant matters. The whole great heart of the summer was the harvest, and the nearer it came the more hugely it loomed. The farm lay cloaked in golden plenty and the fullness of the coming harvest rested upon it like a blessing. In every direction Addie could see it — in the yellow grain that stretched to where the sky started, in the ripe corn that was already being cut and shocked, in the kitchen garden she and Rose-Anne tended, where each stalk and tendril was bent under the weight of ripening vegetables.

These days she scarcely saw her sister except at this gardening chore. Rose-Anne was gone at first light, and although she was in and out of the house a dozen times a day, still she could seldom stop to talk, for some new task always claimed her before Addie could open her own mouth. Rose-Anne had even, one hot day, undertaken the hard dusty job of flax-breaking, had come indoors with specks in her hair and all down the front of her dress, holding in her hand a bunch of pale gray fibers and crying exultantly, "Look, Addie, look what came from the stalks — isn't it beautiful?"

And Addie was busy herself. Every day now she spent hours with old Jeremiah, exercising his withered legs, applying hot towels, massaging. With Abel and Jonah West out of the house most of the time, concentrating on the troubles of the new town site, she had time to spare to devote to her grandfather in complete privacy. She had thought, when she had undertaken his care, that some intimacy might evolve from the situation, that he might even guess who she was, so that she could admit it in a quiet natural way. But surprisingly, this did not happen. It seemed that the old man was full of such concentration, such unshakable determination, that he did not think about her at all. His will power astounded her. He wanted to walk more than anything, and he seemed to see her as an instrument of that aim, but nothing more. I think my mother had that sort of will, Addie reflected once. I think she knew what she wanted too, and would not budge.

Sometimes Addie felt almost fearful of what lay ahead. With summer ending and with her grandfather walking again — she always pictured the two things happening together — everything would be different. First of all, she and Rose-Anne would at last introduce themselves to him. But more, it would be time to think about leaving the farm and heading back toward Philadelphia and the theater season. Every time she thought of the theater and of Billy and Maybelle, who must surely be heading eastward now with the troupe as the summer tour wound to a close, she felt such pangs of love and homesickness she could hardly bear it. She was not unhappy here, not at all, but she did not totally belong and she knew it. Then a day of decision came.

"I have something to show you," she said, standing in the dining room doorway and smiling at Abel Drummond.

Abel looked up from a letter he was writing. His own face, which had more lines in it, Addie thought, than earlier in the summer, was distracted, but he smiled faintly at her and said in an absent-minded way, "Yes? What is it, my dear?"

"Cousin Abel, I know I'm being a nuisance and I know

141

you're at work, but this is something I have to show you," Addie said.

He put down his goose quill pen and replied, "Then if you have to show me, I consider that I have to see it. Bring it on."

"Well, I'm afraid I can't do that. Not yet. But if you could spare a minute to come with me — "

"You are a very mysterious young lady," Abel said. He put both hands on the table and pushed himself up. It was a tired gesture, but Addie was too excited to take much note. Her cousin and Jonah West too had returned the night before from more than two weeks of traveling and she supposed he must still be road-weary. But she knew what she had to show him would be the best lift of all for his spirits.

"Now follow me," she ordered, and he obeyed, walking with her to the stairway and up to the door of old Jeremiah Drummond's room.

Abel frowned. "Nothing's wrong with Uncle, is it?"

"Nothing in the world," she said happily, and pushed him inside the room.

The old man was sitting in his chair by the window with a light cover over his legs. He wore his nightgown and shawl and looked as usual except for a slightly stiffened back and a hand that gripped a walking stick tightly beside the chair.

"Morning, Uncle Jeremiah," Abel said pleasantly. "Now pray tell me. Are you in on this great secret, whatever it is?"

The old man looked at him but said nothing. Addie reached down and plucked the comforter from his legs, and slowly, carefully, he stood up. Leaning on his walking stick, he crossed the room with wavering but determined steps and said casually, "Good morning, Nephew. The weather appears to be holding fine for the crops, does it not?"

Abel reached out to steady the old man, but his help was not needed. Jeremiah Drummond turned, and with Abel hovering beside him, walked back to his chair and sat down.

Addie, nervous with pride and delight, looked at her cousin. Abel's eyes had gone wide with disbelief. He looked at her in a stunned way and shook his head from side to side.

"Uncle Jeremiah," he said weakly, "I can't believe this. I can't believe what my own eyes tell me."

"Lazarus raised, eh, Nephew?" the old man chuckled.

"No less a miracle," Abel agreed. "And do you mean to tell me that you and this young lady have been practicing all this time?"

A dreadful apprehension struck Addie that in his surprise and pleasure Abel might blurt out who she was. Oh, she was ready to tell, right enough, but Rose-Anne must be with her and it was going to be in a special setting that she had pictured a hundred times. Just at twilight and before the candles were brought. And there would be only the three of them present, with her grandfather in his chair and she and Rose-Anne on each side. She looked worriedly at Abel but he merely smiled at the old man in the chair and moved his head slowly in that unbelieving way.

"Wait till old Patchett sees this," he murmured.

"I have been anticipating that moment for a long time," old Jeremiah grinned.

They stayed with him a short while and then helped him back into bed. When they were downstairs, Abel turned to her and said, "Little Cousin, you're a wonder. Not one of us ever thought we'd see him walk again. Your faith was greater than ours."

Addie looked down, not out of modesty but overcome by a sudden fullness of emotion.

"You'll tell him now, won't you?" Abel said softly. "Who you are?"

"Yes," she answered in a small voice. "Now I will tell him. I know nothing can hurt him now. I think he's grown stronger inside as well as in his limbs."

And she excused herself and went hurrying out of the house because all at once she felt unable to contain her joy within its walls. She wanted to get away, out into the open, and she wanted to talk to someone, but not to someone who would answer. Just to someone who would listen and hear how happy she was without demanding any explanation. On a run she headed up the slope toward the high meadow and General Strong's pasture.

She was looking down watching her footing and her thoughts were an excited jumble, so she was almost to the rail fence before she raised her head and looked about. And it was then that she saw the dim-witted boy who lived with Florinda. He was inside the fence close to General Strong. One hand, in fact, lay on the General's handsome neck. The other held something that flashed as the sun caught it — a long-bladed wicked-looking knife.

Addie let out a scream.

"Get away from my horse, you! Get away from him!"

And she reached down to pick up a stick, a stone, a rock, any object to use as a weapon. But before she could lay hand to anything the boy, ducking his head and swinging his arms, turned and made off with surprising speed. Addie found a small round stone and hurled it after him but it fell short. She scrambled through the fence to the General and immediately began looking him over. His eyes had rolled a little wildly at her shouting, but now he grew calm as she touched him. She ran her hands over his neck, his sides, down his flanks. She lifted his feet, looked into his eyes and mouth. He stamped once or twice and shook his head at the fuss. Then she circled around and examined his tail. And it was there that she found the damage. A small bunch of hairs had been cut from his fine tail. Without even a farewell to the General Addie turned and climbed back through the fence and strode off around the hill to the meadow where the log house stood. She was flushed and panting when she got there. The boy was nowhere in sight. She raised her hand and knocked on the door so smartly that her knuckles tingled. Florinda answered after a moment, squinting and scowling into the sunlight.

"Yes? What is it? Oh, it's you."

"Where is that boy of yours?" Addie demanded, breathing hard.

"Nathan? He's about somewhere. You're all of a lather, girl."

"That boy — that wicked boy has hurt my horse. He was up there in the pasture with a knife. I won't have it."

"How did he hurt your horse?"

"He damaged the General's tail," Addie said.

"Oh, pshaw, that wouldn't hurt him."

145

"Did you know about it?"

Florinda shifted her feet about. "There's powerful magic in the tail of a white horse."

"You sent him to do it!"

"I don't see why a person should be so small-minded — "

"General Strong is a theater horse," Addie said with dignity. "He performs. He waltzes and lifts his hooves to march and he can bend his front legs to bow when the audience applauds. I don't want him bothered."

"If I'd known you were the niggling sort that would count the hairs in a horse's tail — "

"Never mind that! He's not to go near that horse again!"

An explosion of laughter from somewhere behind Florinda made Addie jump. She peered past the woman into the dim interior of the little house. There leaning back against the wall in one of the straight chairs was Jonah West. His careless lounging attitude, his unkempt appearance and the rude laughter fanned Addie's temper into a blaze.

"I don't see where this is any of your affair, Mr. West!" she shouted. "Perhaps if you spent more time taking care of the business you were hired to tend, my cousin's affairs would be in a healthier state!"

"Oh, I do appreciate that suggestion, Miss Trimble," he said with elaborate courtesy. "But I long since stopped worrying about any state of health but my own."

"That is quite apparent." Addie turned to Florinda. "Now kindly remember what I've said, Madam. If it happens again I shall feel obliged to report it to my cousin Mr. Abel Drummond." And she turned and stalked off. The mocking voice came behind her.

146

"Hold up there, Miss Trimble. I was just leaving. We'll walk along together."

Addie pursed her lips and refrained from retorting that she would as leave walk with Beelzebub.

"I really don't know," he went on, "what we poor souls ever did around here before you came. How did we manage without you to take charge and tell us all what to do?"

Addie kept looking straight ahead and marching along the narrow path, but he caught up with her, tramping through the meadow grass and stamping down daisies with abandon.

"I shall be starting back to Drummondtown in an hour's time. Will that be sufficient for you to give me my orders and outline my duties? Obviously you know much more about them than I do."

"I never said that," she snapped. She gave him a sideways glance and saw with alarm that he was carrying a small cruet like the one she had emptied earlier in the summer. "It merely seems to me that idling about for the better part of the day hardly becomes a man of affairs."

"Ah, you sadden me. I count heavily on your good opinion," he lamented. "And it's most ungracious of you too, for as it happens I was just about to offer you a present. Something I brought with me from this last trip." And he dug into his shirt pocket and pulled out a folded paper. "There, now. I knew that would interest you."

Addie took it because he thrust it in front of her but she kept up her steady pace.

"Go ahead, look at it."

She unfolded it grudgingly. It was a handbill from the Bowen company, now working its way eastward, as she had

147

suspected, and advertising an appearance for this week in the village of Dingman's Grove. She knew, for she had heard it mentioned, that it was not many miles distant. Yet it might as well be the width of New York state, she thought glumly. Goodness knows she had no wish to run into Bowen again, but the thought of all her old friends, especially Billy and Maybelle, was a painful thrust. She ran her eyes down over the type. "The Incomparable Mrs. Sweeney and the Risible Mr. Buncombe, in new Offerings never before Witnessed West of Philadelphia, direct from their Triumphs in the Chestnut Street Theater — " Addie swallowed with difficulty, her anger dissolved in sudden sadness. And then she glared at the man walking with her. Why else had he brought this if not to hurt her? To mock her and laugh at her?

"Brings back memories, I daresay," he said.

"Yes, indeed. Most pleasant ones," she answered in an offhand way, as if the whole thing were of very little account. If a reaction of some sort was what he was waiting for he would be disappointed.

"I thought it would."

She glanced again at the cruet that dangled from his hand, bumping against his leg as he walked.

"I trust that isn't something you're planning to give my grandfather," she said with a stern look.

His eyebrows went up. "How's that? Oh, this? I don't know. Florinda's always mixing up some mess or other."

"Because I don't think he should be given anything but Mrs. Upjohn's cooking, which I trust."

"Oh. Are you in charge of that too?"

She flushed. "No, and I never pretended to be. But I

148

think I have been helpful to Mr. Jeremiah Drummond."

He dropped the artificial tone he had used earlier.

"He'll need more than your help, little lady."

"Is that so? Thank you for your opinion. Perhaps you'd be interested to hear then that Mr. Drummond is now able to walk with the aid of a stick. My cousin Abel saw it himself today and pronounced it a miracle."

And then an odd thing happened. Jonah West's face turned a dark angry red and with his free hand he grabbed her by the shoulder and spun her around to face him, nearly knocking her off balance and making her gasp with surprise.

"What do you mean — walk? By himself, you mean?"

Addie shook off his grasp as if it had been the touch of a serpent and replied, "As I said, with the aid of a stick. And if I may say so, your attitude — "

"Well, now you've done it," he snapped. "You couldn't keep your sticky fingers and your long nose out of things, could you? You couldn't leave well enough alone. What do you think this is — one of your twopenny-threepenny stage shows? You've meddled in something you know nothing about." And he strode away angrily with the cruet whacking about his leg.

He was walking so fast she could not overtake him, and by the time she reached the house she saw that he had gone back to the barn and was saddling his horse. Within minutes he had pounded down toward the road and galloped off. Her mood, which had been so exultant that she could hardly contain it within her skin only minutes before, had turned black with dread. She was weighed down with the feeling of forces and wills contending around

149

her in some way that she had no knowledge of and was helpless to understand. Tears welled up in her eyes and ran down her cheeks and she dashed them away angrily with her apron. Never mind what Jonah West said. She had seen the look on her grandfather's face when he took those first trembling steps on his own and no one could ever convince her it had been a wrong thing for her to do, to help him to that moment. But the beautiful feeling was gone; the day was ruined for her. Nor was her mood improved when she glanced out toward the barn and saw Rose-Anne standing there in her blue dress, a basket over her arm. She must have been gathering eggs. Her blond hair blew softly in the faint breeze and caught the sunlight to frame her head in a hazy way. Philip Hess was with her. He held Rose-Anne's free hand in both of his; he seemed to be looking earnestly into her eyes. Addie turned and slammed into the house.

She was too angry and unhappy to suggest, when twilight came, that she and Rose-Anne go to their grandfather and have their talk. Instead she went upstairs early and, when Rose-Anne followed her later, scarcely spoke except in grunts, climbing into bed and pretending to be tired. Rose-Anne moved about the room dreamily and did not seem to notice.

Reality, sanity, calmness, returned the next morning as they had a way of doing. Old Jeremiah greeted her cheerfully when she took him his tray. Mrs. Upjohn in the kitchen pressed a fresh berry tart on her for breakfast. Rose-Anne leaned over her shoulder and asked if she felt rested.

150

"You looked so peaked last night. Addie. I think you've overdone."

Addie swallowed the tender crust of the tart and admitted she had been weary, and with remorse remembered how she had even resented Rose-Anne because of the spiteful things Jonah West had said and the ugly mood he had put her in.

"I'll help you in the garden later," she mumbled.

"No, indeed. Not today. You stay indoors and rest."

Her sister's generosity was a whiplash across Addie's back. But before she could answer and insist that she was fine, the kitchen door burst open and Caroline Drummond sailed in, her eyes glowing sparks of joy.

"Girls, girls, wonderful news!" she cried.

She had never called them "girls" before. It had a strangely comradely sound.

"Oh, do tell us, Cousin Caroline," Rose-Anne said.

"I have begged and *begged* my husband to allow me a visit with my sister in Philadelphia," Caroline bubbled. "Only last night he finally agreed. I've scarcely slept a wink thinking of it. And I was up before first light to pack my trunk. Oh, not that I shall take a full wardrobe, but one does need afternoon dresses in the city, for calling and for receiving."

"Oh, how splendid, Cousin Caroline. Are you going at once?" Rose-Anne asked.

Addie was trying to look bright and joyous but the name Philadelphia struck her with cold homesickness just as the Bowen handbill had yesterday when Jonah West had thrust it at her.

"Yes, at once. I'm very nearly ready. My husband will

151

take me into Barker Mills to meet the through stage which is due about noon."

"Noon! Oh my, then you must let me help you," Rose-Anne said, and she and Caroline moved out of the kitchen and up the backstairs. Caroline's high excited voice could be heard all the way up.

"Well! Going to have a little peace and quiet around here," Mrs. Upjohn said, reaching for the teapot.

Addie nodded and tried a smile. Mrs. Upjohn glanced at her. "Makes you think of home, eh, dearie?" she said kindly.

"A little, yes," Addie admitted.

Mrs. Upjohn reached out and gave her hand a pat. "Come on, now, let's you and me have us some more tea and another one of them tarts. And then why don't you sing me that song I fancy so much, 'Blue Are My True Love's Bonnie Eyes'?"

Addie managed a small smile this time in spite of her dark mood. She had certainly never worked for a better audience than Mrs. Upjohn.

The afternoon did a great deal to restore her mood. Once Abel and Caroline had left in a flurry of wraps, trunks and farewells the house was blissfully quiet. Addie spent some time with her grandfather and then, since Rose-Anne had offered her the excuse, rested luxuriously in her room, feeling somewhat sinful at lolling through the green and golden hours. Late in the afternoon she went down to join Mrs. Upjohn in the kitchen. Rose-Anne was there too, helping to roll out a crust for pot pie, and both of them looked toward Addie anxiously as she opened the door. Goodness, she thought with some amusement, did I really look so dreadful before?

"Well, now!" she said. "I must say I feel properly rested at last."

"Oh, Addie, I am relieved," Rose-Anne said. "Come and sit down. Mrs. Upjohn has a lovely supper planned. Just us — and Philip of course — for Cousin Abel won't return until late. He's calling on Judge Perry over eastward. There now. How does that look, Mrs. Upjohn?"

"Lovely, dearie. Now put it in the pan the way I showed you."

"Listen!" Addie raised her head. "Someone's coming." Coming at a fast gallop too, the way it sounded. Not Abel Drummond; he had taken a wagon for Caroline's luggage. This was someone on horseback and coming like the wind. Jonah West returning? Addie prayed not. She had had enough of him to last for some time. She hurried to the back door which stood open to the late sunlight. Outside the long arm of the wellsweep cast a still longer shadow across the dooryard. Up toward the barn Philip Hess trudged with a milk pail in each hand. The sound of the hooves grew louder as the horse turned off the road and galloped up the sloping lane. Addie's spirits sank as it came in sight. That was certainly Jonah West's big brown gelding. But that was not Jonah sliding off and tearing toward the house. It looked more like — yes, it was the young German, Otto Langen. His fair hair had come loose from its leather thong and hung about his shoulders in a wild tangle. Sweat beaded his forehead.

153

"Please, Miss, will you come?" he gasped without even a greeting. "My wife — Elsa — she wants you. She needs you bad."

15

"ALL RIGHT, see here now. Let's not go thrashing around like pigs in a wallow." Mrs. Upjohn spoke in a firm voice but she was nervous herself, Addie could tell. She wiped her hands on the front of her apron and began slapping the pot pie together with large careless motions. She had already pressed a mug of cold buttermilk on the young man and he sat there drinking it greedily yet jumping up every few seconds to pace across the kitchen and back.

"I can do nothing for her," he said in despair. "And I fear she may die."

"Oh, nonsense," Addie said, feeling a chill start up along her arms at his words. "There are women there to help her, aren't there?"

"Yes, there are women, but it does not seem to go right. She feels you are her friend. If you were there — "

"I'll come and gladly," Addie said. "But I don't know anything about such things — about birthing babies — "

"I'll come with you," Rose-Anne offered.

Mrs. Upjohn interrupted impatiently, "Ain't either one of you could hatch a chick from a cracked egg. I've had four of my own and helped my sister to birth seven. I'm the one should go. But someone's got to stay and look after old Mr. Drummond — do the cooking and all. She ain't worth anything," she flung out worriedly as Essie came in from the kitchen garden with a bunch of carrots in each hand.

Rose-Anne frowned as she thought.

"Let me stay then. I'm a good enough cook now to manage. And Essie will help me. You and Addie go, Mrs. Upjohn. I'll explain it to Cousin Abel when he comes back tonight. I'm sure he'd say you should go. Oh, please do. Maybe you can help her."

"Well, I don't know but what that would be best," Mrs. Upjohn muttered. "How are we to go, though? Mr. Drummond's taken the wagon."

"What about the light rig, the one Cousin Caroline takes to church on Sundays? We'll hitch General Strong to it and Mr. Langen can ride the horse he came on." Addie turned to the young German. "Go and rub your horse down and water him, but carefully, Mr. Langen, while we get ready. Let him rest a little; he's been ridden hard. Give him something to eat too. What do we need, Mrs. Upjohn?"

"Well, sheets and clean linen, to start with, and I don't know but what some food would come in handy too. You, girl," she ordered Essie, "get into the cool room there and bring me whatever's on the shelves. Bread, eggs — throw those carrots in too; you can pull more. Is there decent water there at least?" she asked Otto Langen severely.

"Yes, we have water," he said with a one-sided smile.

156

"Not much more, but we have water." And he hurried out to see to the horse.

General Strong rolled his eyes wildly as Addie backed him between the traces of the light carriage, but she kept a firm hand on him and refused to allow any display of temperament.

"I don't care whether you like it or not," she said. "It won't hurt you. We all have to do things we don't care for sometimes. Now that will be all," she ordered as he stamped his front foot down hard. He allowed himself to be backed into the traces but his eyes rolled once again as he caught sight of Mrs. Upjohn's imposing figure with its skirts, shawl, bonnet and reticule. Addie broke off a light switch of elm sapling and held it menacingly and he grew quieter.

Otto Langen rode up on the brown gelding as Addie climbed in after Mrs. Upjohn and picked up the reins.

"Isn't that Mr. West's horse?" she asked.

"I borrowed it, yes."

"He's at Drummondtown then?"

"Yes. He rode there yesterday."

Addie clamped her jaws together. Well, so be it. If she found it necessary to deal with him on top of everything else, she didn't know but what she'd be up to it.

"I believe we're ready, Mr. Langen," she said. "You may lead the way. But please go more slowly now so that we can keep up."

They jounced along for hours, following after the brown horse, and as night fell and the moon rose, Addie felt her hands growing numb from the pressure of the reins and her backside aching mightily from the bumps. Mrs. Upjohn took the whole thing better than Addie would have anticipated, and as the hours wore away she dredged up out of memory a wealth of clinical details regarding her sister's seven confinements. But Addie gave her scant attention. Her mind raced ahead to Drummondtown and she tried to picture what it would be like. Of course it would be the roughest kind of frontier settlement, she was prepared for that. The cabins would be crude and all traces of refinement lacking. No doubt proper streets would not be laid out yet, and she was sure from what she had seen of the Langens that there would not be enough food. However, at least part of their route lay along a broad cleared trail which she surmised was a stretch of the new road to the town and this at least was encouraging. The General, after his first skittishness, was trotting along willingly.

At last they came into a small clearing where a number of tree stumps stood out in the moonlight and cast stubby black shadows. Close to the trail stood two log cabins, roughly made as Addie could see even in this light. They were rectangular in shape and windowless. Otto Langen pulled his horse up and came around to Addie's side of the rig.

"I don't mind going ahead, Mr. Langen," Addie said, although she felt black and blue. "Please don't stop on account of us."

"We are here," he said. "This is it."

Addie and Mrs. Upjohn looked at the two bleak cabins, the stumpy clearing.

"This is Drummondtown?" Addie said.

But the young husband was already dismounting anxiously.

"Please. I will see to the horses in a moment. I must see if it goes well with my wife first."

"Yes, surely," Addie said. "Please go ahead. We'll follow you directly." But when he was gone she and Mrs. Upjohn exchanged a look of disbelief. "I thought there were thirty-nine people living here," Addie said.

"If there are, they're stacked pretty close," Mrs. Upjohn observed dryly. "Well, no matter about that. We got our work cut out for us. You're more limber than me, dearie. Come around to my side and give me a hand."

They unloaded their gear and made their way to the first cabin where Otto Langen had disappeared. It took them a few minutes and he was already on his way back when they reached the door.

"She does no better," he said worriedly. "But I told her you were here, and it gave her great joy. Come this way, please."

The smell hit them first in a fetid wave. Unwashed bodies mostly, Addie surmised. She could see the people only as dim shapes stretched out on the floor of the cabin; the floor itself was hard-pounded dirt. A child was crying somewhere. The place was lighted at one end where a single candle was stuck in the wall, and there a blanket had been thrown over a line for privacy. Otto Langen led them toward it. Mrs. Upjohn held Addie's hand tightly in hers, but she did not waver. Her feet stepped firmly around the pallets and quilts on the floor. The young man held the blanket aside for them and by the candle's wavering light they could see the girl lying on a straw tick on the floor. Two women were with her, standing in hunched, stoic attitudes; they offered no greeting. Addie dropped down beside Elsa and seized her hand. The girl turned toward her. Her face and hair were soaked with sweat, her eyes sooty with pain. She gave a little cry as she recognized Addie.

"Elsa, how good to see you again!" Addie said, thinking as soon as the words were out how fatuous and artificial it sounded. She added more softly, "Oh, Elsa, does it hurt you?"

The girl's eyes grew suddenly wide and her mouth opened and gaped with pain. Behind Addie Mrs. Upjohn asked sharply, "How long has she been like this?"

"Since this morning," Otto answered. "The women say leave her alone, the baby will come. But I cannot. I have fear for her. I am certain she needs help."

Addie liked him for his fear, and she saw Mrs. Upjohn place a comforting hand on his arm.

"Can't see a blessed thing here," she said. "Bring some candles. They're with that gear we brought. We'll want water too."

The two women glared resentment at her, keeping their hands folded across their fronts. They were thin and gaunt, hair pulled back into tight knots. Mrs. Upjohn, plump, hearty and capable, would be more than a match for them, Addie guessed.

"All right now," Mrs. Upjohn said as Otto left. "Let's see what's amiss around here." And she untied her bonnet strings and laid aside her reticule. Addie, holding tight to the girl's hand, felt the reassurance of a commanding presence. Mrs. Upjohn would know what to do. And only as the woman knelt down on the dirt floor, huffing and

160

groaning with the effort, did Addie catch a look of troubled uncertainty that flickered across the plump homely face. Fear turned in Addie's stomach. What if there were nothing Mrs. Upjohn could do after all? But the look vanished as if Mrs. Upjohn had willed it away, and now she placed both hands on Elsa's swollen abdomen and said, "All right now, dearie, you and me have a job to do, haven't we?"

The girl turned toward her voice and Addie could see her trying to read meaning into words she did not understand. But she gave a faint nod of her head, and Addie thought that perhaps it was not too difficult after all to get the hang of a language like Mrs. Upjohn's.

"Now what I think is, that baby might be skewed around crooked," Mrs. Upjohn whispered to Addie. "Either that, or she's so scairt herself she's all tensed up in a knot. If the baby's crooked we may be in for a little trouble, although my sister's fourth come that way and no harm done. But if it's just that she's all pinched up and afeard, might be we can help some. You stick by her and keep talking to her. Now dearie — " She turned back to Elsa and spoke with assurance. "Here's what I want you to do. Next time a pain comes, breathe in and out good and strong."

Addie kept a tight hold on the girl's hand. "Do what Mrs. Upjohn says," she told her. And then, because she thought Elsa had not understood, breathed in and out vigorously to illustrate. The girl nodded weakly. Addie took a handkerchief from her pocket and wiped the sweaty forehead. They were in for a long night of it unless she missed her guess.

16

Dawn hung in a gray mist over the rough clearing and Addie shivered as she opened the door to daylight. Inside the windowless cabin it was still night; the candles flickered and sputtered and dripped lower at the far end where the blanket still hung. There were shadowy silhouettes behind it. Addie, glancing back over her shoulder, could see Mrs. Upjohn's bulky outline as she bent to tuck clean linen around the straw tick. A baby's wail, surprisingly hearty, made Addie smile even though she was chilly, bone-weary and hungry. Everyone else had left the cabin and she could see them now, mostly women and children, huddled around breakfast fires in the clearing. Apparently the second cabin was where most of the men slept.

Otto Langen, who was sitting with his back against a big tree butt, his arms around his knees, had looked up wearily as the door opened, and now he leaped to his feet and ran to her.

"Your wife has a little boy, Mr. Langen," Addie said quickly.

"Does everything go well with her?" he asked.

"Just fine."

His whole body seemed to slump with relief and a smile spread across his face.

"You may go in and see her now."

Addie watched him hurry toward the far end of the cabin, then turned back and took deep breaths of the damp air. She was joined in a moment by Mrs. Upjohn, who looked, in spite of the long journey and the night's vigil, lively and energetic.

"There, now," she said. "You wouldn't have thought that little girl could birth such a stout-looking baby, would you?"

"I do hope he stays so," Addie said doubtfully, with a glance around her at the rough littered cabin.

"Well, one thing at a time," Mrs. Upjohn replied.

"You should rest for a spell," Addie advised, "and perhaps I can cook up some of that food we brought."

Mrs. Upjohn inclined her head in a nod toward the clearing.

"Looks as if somebody's already thought of it."

One of the two gaunt women from the night before was walking toward them with a wooden bowl in each hand. She held the bowls out shyly and the look was a strange sharp reminder of the girl she must have been once before hunger and endless toil changed her into something different. Addie and Mrs. Upjohn took the bowls and thanked her and she walked away quickly. It was a thin gray porridge she had brought them and it tasted like sawdust, but they were hungry enough to eat it. When the young husband returned his face was shining with relief.

"I thank you both, ladies," he said formally. "My wife thanks you too."

"Oh, pshaw." Mrs. Upjohn waved him away. "I'm going to see about giving that baby a proper bath now." And she bustled off heavily.

"Is Mr. West still here, Mr. Langen?" Addie asked.

"I saw him this morning, yes."

"Where is he now, do you think?"

Otto Langen raised a hand to point. "There, with those men. By the big stump, you see?"

Addie followed the gesture and nodded.

"I must go to my work now. Will you return home at once?"

"Yes, soon. A little later in the day."

He nodded and went out, still beaming. Addie stood in the doorway observing the group of men clustered around an enormous stump that had been left in the clearing. Now by daylight she could see that a third cabin was being built a short distance away and that logs stood piled for a fourth one near it. The giant stump would have to be dug out, it seemed, to make room for this.

She considered whether to speak with Jonah West, but decided against it. She had nothing to say to him — nothing, certainly, that she could discuss calmly. Better if she returned home and took the whole matter up with her cousin Abel who obviously could stand some honest reporting on how matters really stood at the town. All around her she could see signs of inefficiency, slovenly management and a manner of living so primitive that it could certainly produce nothing but suffering and disease. If this was the great enterprise that Abel was pouring money and effort into, he had best look to it himself and not leave it in the hands of someone as careless and offhand about it as Jonah West. Addie felt heartsick at the thought that the new life that had entered the cabin in the night hung by a most precarious thread.

There was a shout from the direction of the big stump, and she watched as the men formed themselves into two lines and began pulling on heavy ropes that were fastened to the stump. It was a job normally done by a team of oxen with chains, but there were no oxen here. The men heaved and strained at the ropes and it startled her to see that Jonah West was pulling along with the others. He shouted orders, directing them as they worked in unison. Presently they paused and he and another man ran back and began prising at the stump with heavy poles. When they had loosened it more they pulled again. The process was repeated over and over until the stump at last was pulled free. The men gave a mighty shout. Addie turned away and went to help Mrs. Upjohn.

By the time she stepped outside again the baby had been bathed and warmly wrapped in clean linen. Elsa had been made comfortable and the end of the cabin where she lay had been made as neat as possible. Mrs. Upjohn had even swept the dirt floor smooth.

"Now before we go back I'm going to cook up some food for these children," Mrs. Upjohn announced. The two women had joined her now, and she began issuing orders about cooking pots and water which they managed to comprehend in a way that baffled Addie.

The sun had risen higher and the day's heat was beginning to mount. Addie sat in the cabin doorway swatting at flies and gnats that buzzed around her head, feeling the oppressive heavy air. She observed that the crew of men that had been working on the stump was now at the site of the new cabin working with axes and setting the logs straight. Jonah West was with them. He had removed his shirt and she could see that his skin was shiny with sweat as he swung the ax and shouted instructions, showing the men how to make the proper notches in the logs so they would dovetail at the ends. When they had notched a log he took one end of it and, with another man at the other end, swung it into place, lifting, straining, making sure that it set true. He seemed totally preoccupied with what he was doing.

By midafternoon Addie sought out Mrs. Upjohn and suggested that they should be preparing for the trip back. Mrs. Upjohn was by this time surrounded by children lured to her cooking fire in the clearing by the fragrance of stew. She was busy ladling it out. She waved to Addie absent-mindedly and replied, "Just a little while, dearie. Take some of this in to Elsa, why don't you."

This time when Addie returned, Mrs. Upjohn had lined the smaller children in a row and was scrubbing their faces and hands and brushing out tangled hair. Addie glanced toward the men at the new cabin. Jonah West was no longer among them.

There's a stream around here somewhere, she thought, for my grandfather mentioned it. That would be the place for the mill. She walked away from the cabin clearing to look for it. If no one was about, she thought, she could sit on its bank and remove her shoes and stockings, perhaps even wash and refresh herself.

She found it without any trouble, but she was not able to find a quiet spot to sit with her feet in the water; another crew of men was working here, and she recognized Jonah West among them. This group appeared to have tackled the job of putting a footbridge across the stream. They had picked a spot where it narrowed somewhat, running between low banks. A huge tree trunk lay on the ground, a tree so large it looked to Addie as if it had been cut from the stump she had just watched them remove, and three wedges had already been driven into it. Jonah West stood astride it with a heavy wooden maul in his hands, and as Addie shrank back where she would not be seen, he came down with a swift blow on the first of the wedges. The log cracked open and he struck the second one. Further and further he drove the wedges until at last the whole trunk split wide open in a clean break and the two halves lay there rocking, smooth sides upward.

"All right, boys," he shouted. "Somebody get that other end and we'll put 'em across!"

But two men could not lift even a half of the log, so two more came running and the four of them, wading in water almost to their waists, struggling for footing, slipping and thrashing, managed to set it in place. They returned for the second half, and now Addie was holding her breath and straining along with them. But once it was across Jonah West did not appear satisfied with the way the logs were set into the bank and demanded that rocks be brought for reinforcement. By the time the logs were buttressed securely in place and shored up with rocks and mud, all the

167

men were slimy and wet, breathless with fatigue. Addie turned and hurried back to the cabin before anyone could notice she had been watching. When she reached the doorstep she paused and turned back, and after a moment she saw him coming along the footpath toward the clearing. The other men turned off and he continued by himself. His step was weary; his shoulders sagged with an exhaustion that Addie could almost feel in her own arms and legs.

A small child, one of those Mrs. Upjohn had been ministering to, went running across the path in front of him, caught his toe on a root and went down with a mighty wail. Jonah caught him up quickly, swinging him with one motion under his arm and carrying him along like a sack of meal, jiggling him so that the cries turned to shrieks of laughter. After a moment he set the child down, watched the small legs churning away, and then turned to the cabin where Addie stood.

"I heard you were here," he said unexpectedly. "Otto says he has a son." He hesitated and then added, "I'm sure we appreciate your help."

She wondered whether he meant it and thought it odd that he had said "we." She replied, "I've done nothing at all, I'm afraid. Mrs. Upjohn was the one."

They eyed each other warily like cocks in a pit, almost as if each was seeing something in the other that was proving to be a surprise, so that they were not sure what attitudes to strike.

"Mrs. Upjohn cooked up some stew," she said. "I imagine you could use some."

He shook his head. "I'll fix myself something later."

"I never realized how much — " she began. "That is,

there seem to be so many things that must be done all at once in a new settlement."

He nodded slowly. "The trouble is, we aren't even past first things here. Food and shelter. We've got to get more cabins up and we've got to put by all the food we can for winter. Lord knows there's little enough even so. That storm washed away our footbridge and it had to be replaced because we've got some things planted on the opposite bank. Not much, for we didn't have much seed. But corn and a few pumpkins and squash. Be quite a trick to bring 'em all across on our heads, wading."

Remembering what her grandfather had said, Addie remarked, "I thought there would be a mill somewhere along the water. My grandfather said a mill is always first, and the town builds up around it."

His mouth formed a smile but it was one-sided and Addie thought there was no real amusement in it.

"So it should. But this is a town being built hind end first, Miss Trimble. Nothing's right about it, nor hasn't been from the beginning."

"Why?" Addie asked, and her voice had gone small and breathless. She was not sure how ready she was for the answer.

He looked at her, raising one eyebrow in a kind of appraisal.

"Why, because Mr. Abel Drummond is in such an all-fired hurry to become a big man in the state. And a town of his own building — a town named Drummondtown — that'll be a big help to him. So he's doing the whole thing in a rush, hacking a road through, getting all these people here and never mind whether he's got enough to feed them.

Poor city devils, they've been hungry all their lives. They thought it would be different here in this country. The way things stand, it seems to me the best thing would be for them to go to the Quaker settlement for the cold months. At least they'd eat and have shelter there. But Abel won't hear of it. Of course if things get bad enough, he may not be able to stop them."

Addie's knees began to feel watery. Still she felt compelled to argue.

"It seems to me that isn't very loyal of you, Mr. West. I mean, my Cousin Abel is your employer. If you disapprove of him so much — "

"He's not my employer!" Jonah burst out. "Maybe he gives the orders right now, but I've never felt I worked for him. Old Mr. Drummond's who I work for, and as far as loyalty's concerned, that's where mine lies and nowhere else."

"Then why were you so upset and so — rude the other day when I told you I'd helped him to walk? You acted as if I'd done something dreadful."

His face turned worried. "I'm sure you didn't mean to, Miss. I apologize for flying off at you that way. But it worried me, you see, hearing that. I don't like the idea that Abel knows he can walk — that he's getting stronger all the time."

"Why?"

He turned away from her, moving his head from side to side, and then suddenly he swung back to face her.

"Oh, Lord, can't you see it? Because Abel wants him dead, that's why!"

Addie reeled back as if she had been poleaxed.

"Wants him dead!"

"Abel's up to his neck in debts. He's borrowed from everybody from here to the Pennsylvania line, and a lot of it's been wasted too. I shouldn't have yelled at Otto as I did when he told me about the cattle, but I blame myself for those oxen being slaughtered. I should have known these people were starting to get desperate. But I just didn't think of it. It never occurred to me they'd do such a thing. I was off that week begging and bargaining for tools and cooking pots; we haven't even enough of those."

"Wants him dead!" Addie repeated stupidly. "But what would that — how would that — "

"Abel's his heir," Jonah West said grimly. "He came to the old man a few years back — had this plan in mind right along — and he's managed to pull it off. Your grandfather was one of the most important men in this part of the country. Abel moved right in and sympathized with him about his daughter running off and marrying a dancer — not to say anything against your father, Miss. Then when the illness struck, Abel settled in for good — took the reins right over. Your mother, she would have been the one to inherit everything, but when she died, that changed it all. It put Abel in a good position. Only when you and your sister showed up — Well, all he could do was try not to panic. Most of all, not let the old man know who you were."

"But then perhaps I should have told my grandfather?"

"Yes, perhaps I should have too. But at first I did fear for his life — he was such a frail peaked old thing until lately. And I worried about what Abel might do — what move he might make if the whole kettle was brought to a boil that way."

Addie was listening to him, but she was also remembering Abel's soft words two days earlier. *You'll tell him now, won't you? Who you are?*

"What he might do?" she echoed hollowly.

Jonah shook his head impatiently as if to clear it.

"I don't know," he said. "Perhaps he wouldn't do anything. Not to really hurt the old man, that is. But he's so set in his mind about this town, he doesn't seem to care what it costs — in money or in anything else. He doesn't care a hang about people, you see. Even his wife, poor woman; he gives no more thought to her than to a stick of furniture. She's a fool in many ways, but I can't help pitying her. She hasn't had an easy life either."

"Mr. West, you're frightening me. And I know you're frightened yourself."

Jonah West took several nervous pacing steps back and forth. Addie could hear water squishing in his sodden boots.

"Well, I am. Right now, just this week, something big is coming up that could mean a great deal to Abel. He's been corresponding with a man back in the Hudson Valley — a Dutchman, Jan Vreeland. He's rich, and he's shown an interest in investing in western land. Now he's on his way out here. Abel expects him within the week. It looks as if he might make Abel an offer. Perhaps he'd even take over Abel's debts for a share of the land and the town. I don't know. But he's mighty everlasting rich, and that's what Abel's needed all along. He has the land. He needs cash. But Vreeland's a businessman, and cagey. He'll ask about

172

title to the land. He'll want to see proof that Abel's the true owner. And how can Abel show him that unless — "

Addie picked up her skirts and mounted the cabin doorstep.

"I must get back at once," she said. "I'll get Mrs. Upjohn and start back right away."

"Hold on now; wait a minute. Philip's there, isn't he? Philip's a good steady fellow. And your sister too? No harm can come to him with the two of them right there."

"Oh, I know. I'm sure you're right. But I feel I should be there too. I want to go back."

He studied her for a moment. "Then I'll go with you."

"There's no call for that. You've got your hands full here. Mrs. Upjohn will be with me."

"I want to go," he said.

Addie did not answer at once. Instead, she looked down toward the ground, a little away from him. Finally she said haltingly, "Mr. West, I'm afraid I've done you a great wrong I thought you were unfeeling about these people. And maybe even — dishonest. I want to apologize."

His eyes showed a glimmer of amusement through their weariness.

"Did you think that for a fact? Well, maybe I am. You still don't know any different."

Addie raised her eyes to his face. She answered slowly, "Yes, I do. I know different. I've seen you working here — harder than anyone should work. I've seen how these people look to you and respect you. And I know that I've been meddling. I've poked in where I shouldn't have. Even with my grandfather — "

"No, don't ever be sorry for that, Miss Trimble," he

173

interrupted. "That was the right thing to do. It's meant a whole new life for him. He'd given up before you came, do you know that?"

"Well, it's no matter now. I just want to get back to him. I'm sure you're right that Philip and Rose-Anne will look after him, but I want to be there." She glanced at his sodden clothes, his muddy boots. "You must put on dry things, Mr. West. And do lie down and rest for just a short time while Mrs. Upjohn and I pack up and get ready. You look poorly. We'll make good time tonight; the moon's nearly full."

"How you do take charge, Miss Trimble," he marveled. "Never mind, I'm just tired enough to let you do it." He turned and started walking with heavy steps toward the other cabin, the one where most of the men were quartered. She watched him go. After a few feet he turned and said, "You could call me Jonah if you'd a mind to. I wouldn't object."

She raised her hand in a timid wave and nodded, then turned and hurried inside.

Organizing Mrs. Upjohn for the trip back was more of a chore than Addie had anticipated. The woman seemed to have several dozen last-minute concerns which needed her attention. Most of them had to do with Elsa and the baby; she left a spate of instructions, none of which, Addie thought, were understood. Yet Elsa smiled broadly and nodded at everything, so how could one be sure? The two thin women, now shadows behind the substantial Mrs. Upjohn, were also given final instructions, mostly concerning the food Mrs. Upjohn was leaving behind and how best to use it so it would go far. There was a small child whose nose ran — Mrs. Upjohn advised a warmer covering at night — and there were any number of admonitions concerning the value of cleanliness in general. Did any of them know the way to make soap? It wanted only a stout kettle, and once you'd gathered up enough good clean ashes — Addie prodded and said they'd best not tarry any longer.

"Oh, dear me, dear me. Yes, well, hitch the horse. I'll be there straightaway."

Addie hurried out and found General Strong in a small fenced enclosure back of the cabin where Otto had taken him. She hitched him to the light rig and led him around front. Then she hailed Otto, just approaching across the clearing with his face washed and hair neatly brushed and clubbed back.

"Mr. Langen!" she called. "I know you're on your way to see your wife and baby. But would you be so good as to go and tell Mr. West first that we're ready to leave?"

"I will, Miss," he replied cheerfully. His attitude indicated he would gladly have gone several miles out of his way to oblige her. She stood and waited while he trotted back toward the other cabin. The General put his head down near her and she patted him absent-mindedly. Mrs. Upjohn worked her way out of the cabin with what seemed a great flurry of shawls and came to join Addie beside the carriage, shaking her head.

"Ain't a thing you could mention that these poor folk aren't without," she said, frowning. "Lord knows what's going to happen to them over the winter — "

"Miss! Ladies!" It was Otto Langen, calling to them as he raced back across the clearing. "Miss, you'd better

175

come. I can't wake him. He's hot, like fire, and his breathing is bad."

Addie and Mrs. Upjohn exchanged a look of alarm and hurried toward the other cabin.

"Well, he ain't going anywheres tonight," Mrs. Upjohn said flatly as she took her hand away from the sick man's forehead and straightened up. A candle stuck in the top of an upended keg was the only light near the lumpy straw pallet where he lay, tossing feverishly back and forth. His eyes rolled back beneath half-closed lids and he spoke now and then in breathless phrases that hissed and mumbled and could not be understood.

"Isn't there something we can do for him?" Addie said, pressing her two hands together tightly.

"There ain't a gre' deal, I don't think, no," Mrs. Upjohn said, shaking her head. "If there was even a little Peruvian bark handy, I could brew it up for him. That would stem a fever, but it ain't likely there's anything like it around here. Maybe cold cloths on his forehead might help some."

Addie took her elbow and drew her aside.

"Mrs. Upjohn, I haven't said anything to you about why I'm anxious to hurry home, but I have some concern for my grandfather."

In the flickering gloom the older woman returned her look with steady eyes that did not question.

"Is that so?"

"Yes. And I still feel I must go. But I just couldn't bear to leave Mr. West here with no one to look after him. Would you stay, just for another day or so? I'm sorry to ask you to do it, but — "

"I'll stay and gladly," Mrs. Upjohn said, not making any more fuss about it, and not asking either why it was suddenly so important to Addie that Jonah West be ministered to.

The thought flickered past Addie briefly, why was it so hard to understand and accept pure goodness? Her eyes misted over and she threw her arms around Mrs. Upjohn.

"Thank you, Mrs. Upjohn. Thank you more than I can say. Someone will come for you. I'll arrange it."

"It's a long trip for you to make alone," Mrs. Upjohn said worriedly.

"I'll be fine."

"Well, then. If you feel you must, you'd best get started. I'll take care of things here. Sometimes these fevers burn out overnight. Let's hope so. Don't you worry about me." And she started removing the top layer of shawls.

"Mr. Langen — " Addie beckoned the young man out of doors and said, "Would you help me? I want to unhitch my horse and saddle him. I can make better time that way. I'll borrow Mr. West's saddle."

"I'll fetch it for you, Miss." He hurried off and she unhitched the General from the small carriage. Otto was back in a moment with the saddle and helped her with it.

"You can ride this way, Miss? One leg on each side?" He blushed a little.

"Yes indeed. There now. Just hold the stirrup for me." And she mounted lightly and tucked her skirts under her. "Mr. Langen, please help care for Mr. West. He's very ill."

He handed her the reins. "Jonah has been good to all of us, Miss. We'll do our best for him. Thank you for coming. Thank you for looking after Elsa."

"Please tell her I'll come back and see her soon."

"I will, Miss. I'll tell her."

The moon was rising, huge and pale, as Addie started off down the trail. The General gave two or three nervous little dancing steps and flattened his ears. She leaned close to speak to him.

"Now, General," she said in a soft cajoling voice, "I want to see your very best performance."

Moon-mist and night air closed around her; wind streaked past her, pulled at her hair and flared the General's tail out behind them as they flew through the dark. General Strong's feet found the way without a fault, dodging loose stones and uneven ground with uncanny skill. Almost, Addie thought, showing off a little, and she bent lower and spoke to him to let him know she had noticed.

"Good boy, General," she said. "Very very clever."

It was late and the house was quiet, sleeping a dark and silent sleep when they arrived back at the farm. She stabled General Strong and tiptoed inside, closing the door behind her softly. Without a candle she crept up the backstairs from the kitchen and pushed open the door of her grandfather's room. Moonlight flooded in over the bed, the woven rag carpet, the chair by the window. She went to the bed and leaned over it. The old man slept with one hand outside the coverlet. The left one, she could see. The one restored; the one that had worked so tirelessly at the ball of clay. She leaned over and listened to his breathing, heard that it was steady and deep. After a few moments she went to her own room. Rose-Anne stirred in her sleep.

"Addie, you're back — "

"Yes."

"Did the baby come?"

"Yes. A little boy."

Rose-Anne made a sound of pleasure and rolled over to her own side of the bed as Addie crept in between the sheets. Addie thought she had gone back to sleep at once, but presently, "You smell of horse," she said sleepily.

17

WEARINESS dragged at Addie like a wet skirt as she went down to the kitchen in the morning. Her eyelids were heavy; her hair was stringy and had resisted the comb. Her sense of well-being was in no way restored by the sight of her sister. Rose-Anne stood in Mrs. Upjohn's place behind the big wooden table, enveloped in a large apron, floury to the elbows, rosy-cheeked and beautiful. Her beauty made Addie feel drab twice over.

"Addie! You shouldn't have come down so early. You must be worn out."

"Have you taken Grandfather his tray? Is he all right?"

"Yes, of course. He's fine." Rose-Anne stared at her. "Why?"

"Where's Cousin Abel?"

"Gone into Barker Mills. He'll be back later in the day."

"Philip's out at the barn?"

"No. Philip's away for a while. Tell me about the baby."

"What do you mean, he's away?"

"He's gone to buy a horse."

"Gone where?"

"Goodness, Addie! North of here somewhere. To some farmer who has horses to sell. He lost one of his work horses this summer. Remember the one that sickened and died? He has to replace it with the harvest coming on."

"When will he be back?"

"In a day or two."

"A day or two! How did he hear about the farmer with the horses to sell?"

"Cousin Abel told him about it. Said he'd better hurry if he wanted a good buy."

Rose-Anne wiped flour from her hands and brought Addie biscuits with golden tops, honey and a pot of tea. "There. Have something to eat. You really look done in."

Addie sank into a chair and tried a bite of biscuit, but it clung to the dry roof of her mouth and she swallowed it in a lump. Her eyes went around the kitchen.

"Where's Essie?"

"Oh, Essie had to go care for her sister's children. Sister's sick."

"When did that happen?"

"I'm not sure. Cousin Abel mentioned it last night." Then, seeing the distress in Addie's face, "But I can manage fine. With so few in the house it's simple."

Addie nodded, starting to feel numb. "Who's doing the chores? The milking and all that?"

Rose-Anne's mouth tightened a little. "Well, now, *that* I don't like too well. But he doesn't come around the house, so I don't even see him except when I go out to feed the chickens and gather eggs."

"Who?"

"Why, that Nathan. That strange boy who hasn't all his wits."

"*He's* here?"

"Yes, but just out at the barn. Cousin Abel says he's handy enough, although Caroline is so scared of him that Abel can't permit him near the place when she's around. Don't you like the biscuits I made?"

Addie moved the plate away from her and folded her hands tightly in front of her on the table to keep them from trembling.

"Rose-Anne," she said, "there's something I have to tell you."

"My dear, if your performance in the theater is equal to your performance in the kitchen, then Philadelphia should be at your feet," Abel Drummond said with a charming little bow toward Rose-Anne across the table from him.

Rose-Anne colored prettily and murmured a denial. Addie marveled at her control. Rose-Anne always did have a way of rising to occasions even though she looked like fluff. A born trouper.

"Now, Addie, tell me how you found things at Drummondtown," Abel said, turning to her with polite interest.

Not a word, Addie reminded herself sternly. Not a word, not a look, not a gesture. Not until I've figured a way to get Grandfather away from here.

"Oh, I found it ever so interesting, Cousin Abel," she said with enthusiasm. "A bit rough, of course — "

"Ah yes, a true frontier town."

"Just so. But full of activity. I found the prospects most stimulating."

"I'm glad to hear you say so. All work progressing apace, I trust?"

"Oh, yes indeed. Work on two new cabins was well advanced, and a footbridge across the stream."

"You saw Jonah there?" It was asked casually but Addie was wary.

"From a distance only," she replied. "I was too occupied with helping Mrs. Upjohn to engage in conversation."

"A most charitable act," he murmured. "Mother and child are well, I trust?"

"Yes, thriving."

"It surprised me that you came home by night," Abel said blandly. "And without the carriage."

Addie was prepared for this. "Mrs. Upjohn felt I should return to help Rose-Anne. But she was determined to stay for a day or two, so I left the carriage for her. She's such a capable person," Addie hurried on, trying to change the subject. "I'm sure her presence there will be most helpful to the settlers."

"Ah yes, an excellent woman." Abel buttered a biscuit. "Have you seen your grandfather?"

Addie stifled a yawn. "Oh dear, I'm afraid I was too exhausted from the ride. Perhaps tomorrow."

They went on chatting companionably through the evening meal until Abel rose, remarking that he'd best see whether Nathan had performed the chores properly.

"The poor boy is willing but lacks the power of concentration," he said, shaking his head.

When he had left Addie and Rose-Anne exchanged worried looks across the table. Rose-Anne said, "Addie, are you sure about all this? In spite of those things Mr. West told you, I have doubts. It's hard for me to believe Cousin Abel means any harm to Grandfather."

"He means it."

"Can he really be that kind of man?"

Addie thought back to Drummondtown, to the bleak stumpy clearing, the crowded cabins, noisome and unclean, to the thin haggard women and the ill-fed children.

"I know what kind of man he is," she said.

"Oh, if only Philip were here!"

"Abel made sure he wouldn't be. That means it's going to be soon."

"What can we do? How can we protect Grandfather?"

"Keep our eyes open every minute. Watch his door. See that Abel doesn't go in there."

"But how can we stop him?"

"I don't know yet. But I know Abel won't want a fuss. Whatever he does, he'll do quietly."

They cleared the table and tidied the kitchen, talking softly as they worked, weighing plans, considering alternatives. Finally, untying her apron, Rose-Anne said, "It would help some if we just had an idea what Abel was planning to do!"

Addie had crossed to the open door to look out. Twilight was gathering in the corners of the kitchen and outside the sky was turning lavender pink. Up by the barn three figures stood — the dim-witted boy Nathan with a milk pail in each hand, Abel Drummond with one foot propped on a large stone, hands on his hips as he talked and, listening to him, nodding slowly, the black-caped figure of Florinda.

Addie turned toward Rose-Anne slowly. "I know what he's planning to do," she said. "He's going to poison him."

"Poison!" Rose-Anne said, and her blue eyes grew wide.

"Shh. Yes. I'm sure of it, for I saw poison in the cabin where that woman Florinda lives. She's got it all right — plenty of it."

"Do you think she's a witch?" Rose-Anne asked.

Addie considered it. She was not quite sure what to think about witches. There were those who did believe in them. And who was to say it was not so? There was the dim-witted Nathan. Might it not be that she had cast a spell on him? Addled his mind and taken away the power of reason?

"I think she could be one," she admitted slowly.

"Then how can we — I mean — she must know powerful magic and spells."

"I'm not worried about spells," Addie said curtly. "Not yet, anyway. It's those jars I saw in her cabin."

"But we take all his food to him."

"I think she may have tried already," Addie said. "She's sent things here and I've dumped them out."

"Then we can dump them again."

"Yes, for a while at least," Addie agreed. "For as long as Abel doesn't suspect we're onto him."

"Don't you think we'd better be upstairs then, nearer to Grandfather?"

"Yes. Come on."

They posted themselves at the window of their own room

185

which commanded a good view of the rear of the house. They watched as the trio by the barn broke up and Florinda and Nathan walked away around the hill toward the little cabin in the meadow. Abel remained outside for a long time as if enjoying the long summer evening. They kept their eyes on him as he walked back and forth in a relaxed way, sometimes with his hands clasped behind his back. There seemed nothing urgent in his manner, or anxious. Then as darkness moved in it became harder to follow his movements.

"Is he still there?" Addie whispered.

"I think he's sitting on the rock."

"But we can't be sure."

"Wait — I'll listen at the door — see if I can hear anything in the house."

Rose-Anne opened the door and stuck her head out. "It seems all quiet."

Addie left the window and joined her. "It's no good," she said. "We can't be sure. I'm going to Grandfather's room."

"Oh, Addie, be careful."

"Wait here. Keep listening."

"All right."

Addie slipped out into the hall and felt her way down it in the warm dark, turning left at the end and groping with her hands flat against the wall for her grandfather's door. When she reached it she felt for the knob and turned it slowly, not making a sound. It was locked, and there was no keyhole in the door. It had been latched from the inside. Addie pressed her ear against the door. At first there was only silence inside, but then she was sure she heard a faint sound of movement. Her throat contracted as a shout leaped up

186

and was stifled. Shouting was no good. It would only advertise her presence. She turned and fled back silently to Rose-Anne.

"Someone's in there with him," she gasped. "The door's locked."

"Abel?"

"I think so. He must have stolen back in the dark. I should have gone and stayed right with Grandfather. Now I've got to get in there some other way."

With the same thought, the two girls ran to the open window and stuck their heads out.

"There isn't any other way," Rose-Anne wailed. "It's around on the other side of the house. You can't even see his window from here."

Addie was silent for a moment, looking down toward the ground and then, slowly, up toward the decorative cornice that ran around the house above their heads. Beyond it the slate roof sloped sharply up to a peak.

"Could I walk around on that cornice, do you think?" she asked.

"Addie — no!"

But Addie thought about it. "Not in these clothes, I couldn't. But wait a minute. Oh dear, we should have brought a light from the kitchen. Never mind, I can find it." She was on her knees rummaging in the clothes chest that was against one wall, searching with her hands for her sailor costume. White trousers, middy blouse, soft black slippers — never mind the blue jacket and the hat. "There," she said, "those will do." And she began unbuttoning her dress with quick fingers. She slipped into the trousers and middy and changed into the soft slippers.

187

"Addie, please don't! How can you get up to the cornice anyway?"

"I'll climb up on the shutter far enough to reach it."

"But maybe the shutter won't hold! Or the cornice either."

"Grandfather built this house himself; you heard Abel say so. I'll bet it's built to last till the Second Coming, cornice and all."

"Addie — I'm scared." Rose-Anne's face was a white blur in the darkness.

"Go throw the latch on the door," Addie ordered. "Don't let anybody in except me."

Rose-Anne nodded and said no more as Addie climbed through the window. She tested the shutter, letting it bear her weight before hoisting herself on it and swinging up over the slight projection of the cornice. Here the slate roof shot up so steeply that it surprised Addie, and for a moment she teetered there holding on to the big brick chimney for support, leaning against it.

"Are you all right?" Rose-Anne's frightened voice came from the window below.

"Yes. I'm fine. Go latch the door."

She heard Rose-Anne's retreating footsteps and for another moment she stood there trying to get her bearings. Yet she felt confused and off balance. Something was happening to her that she had not counted on. A watery weakness made her limp; her knees trembled. She could feel sweat breaking out on her body. Something was draining out of her — courage, instinct, strength. She was not sure where to turn, how to stand, which foot to set down first. And more, she felt the heavy hand of fear on her

— fear of what lay ahead, what evil, danger or death lay around the corner of the house. Without warning her legs buckled under her and she dropped to a crouch, resting her forehead on her knees.

"Papa," she whimpered. "Papa — "

A long dark silence answered her with only crickets and the night wind stirring. And then, out of the darkness, Terence came. Not as a crash, rending the heavens; not as a spectral presence on the battlements like Hamlet's father. But Terence as he had been in life, handsome, slender, light-footed, dancing behind her eyelids. And Terence's voice came, strong and serious, as she had heard it two years before on the first night she had walked the wire with him.

Afraid? Oh, no. It's too late for being afraid, dearie. Our names are on that handbill tacked to the tree out yonder. That's the same as a promise, having your name on a handbill. It means you've promised to appear.

Addie snuffled, clinging to the chimney and brushing away tears. Her name was on no handbill now. But in a way she had promised, even if only herself. She rose cautiously from the crouching position and stood there, leaning against the chimney, feeling the rough brick against her cheek. Moonlight silvered the steep roof but threw the cornice at its edge into a shadow.

You never look with your eyes, love. Feel — with your feet. Back straight, eyes front.

Addie drew herself up.

Arms straight out, wrists relaxed. It throws the hands into a pretty position.

Addie's arms came out at her sides and held there balancing delicately. One foot reached out, toe pointed in

189

its soft black slipper, feeling for a hold. When she was sure of it she brought the other one forward. Weight shifted, balance held. Without hesitation she walked the cornice, a slim figure against the moonlight, all the way around to old Jeremiah's window where, just under her feet, candlelight glowed. She did not look at the ground thirty feet below.

18

⌒⌒

THERE WAS a shutter here too and Addie was able to lower herself from the cornice and grab it between her knees. Now she was strong and sure of her movements and as she swung into position to enter the room feet first, she straightened her legs and pointed her toes as Terence had taught her. She slid in through the open window, landing with a graceful bounce as she had done so many times on stage.

She saw the room in a flashing glance that made it appear like one of Bowen's tableaux. All action was halted for the startled moment of her entrance. It was dark except for a single candle on the bedside table and around this a moth, the only moving thing, was making wild lunges. At the foot of the bed Florinda stood with a cup in her hand. She looked tiny and bent and evil and her black eyes caught the candle flame as she seemed about to move toward the old man propped up on pillows in the bed. It was the cup that Addie's attention focused on.

"Sir! Don't drink anything!" she shouted, and then felt herself grabbed from behind. A hand was clapped over her mouth. By the hard calloused strength of it she was sure it belonged to Nathan. For a moment she was held there pinioned and rigid. Florinda looked at her, eyebrows drawn into a scowl. Old Jeremiah Drummond sat up straight in the bed.

"Keep your voice down, my dear," he said. "You'll spoil everything."

She stared wildly for a moment, then blinked her eyes by way of agreeing, and at a signal from the old man Nathan withdrew his hand and let her go. She ran to the bed and collapsed on her knees beside it.

"You don't understand, sir. I saw them together and she's trying to give you something — "

"Hush. Hark. We must keep our voices low."

"Yes. All right." She dropped her voice. "But she's here to do you in, sir. I saw her talking with Abel. And that cabin of hers is full of poisons in jars. I've seen it. Mandrake, wolfbane, hemlock. Abel's head over heels in debt, you see, and he must have the inheritance right away because some important man from the East is coming to see him soon. That's why he told her — "

"Yes, yes. I know. He gave her two gold coins and said that he wanted a draught from her stock of poisons. Something that would put me to sleep for good."

"Yes! Well, I don't know about the gold, but — "

"And she told him such things were dangerous, that they must be administered cautiously lest suspicion be aroused. Old Patchett is a fool, she said, and a poor excuse for a doctor, but he would know the work of poison. She must

192

give the dose herself, she said, and skillfully. So Abel agreed. And since Nathan goes everywhere she goes, he came along."

Addie looked around the room — first at Florinda, still holding the cup and scowling at her, then at Nathan, standing back near the window, arms swinging, head moving aimlessly in little back and forth motions. And realization struck Addie with peculiar force. She had the thing completely awry. She had not figured it out right at all. Something was wrong here.

"Well, then," she stammered, "what's in that cup?"

"Just camomile tea, my dear," he said, and took it as Florinda held it out to him. He sipped. "I have a fondness for it. But as far as giving me anything harmful, she'd never — the fact is — " He hesitated delicately.

Florinda switched her feet about, shuffling uneasily. Finally she mumbled, "What he means to say is, I be no regular witch at all."

Addie stared at her. "You're not!"

"Well — no. Not so as to say a real true one. Although I do simpling and curing, yes. And a few other sidelines, as you might say. Your simple potions, your philters, yes. I can handle those, and I know some charms and spells such as the country girls ask for. I've done a nice little business in charms and spells. Kept me in fresh eggs."

Addie shook her head slowly in disbelief. "And all those jars and jugs in your house? All those poisons on the high shelf?"

Florinda looked abashed. "Oh, just parsley and self-heal — things like that. I wouldn't — I'd never handle any real poisons. I grow some of 'em in the garden — henbane and deadly nightshade — but it's for show. I wouldn't bring 'em in the house for fear Nathan might take something by mistake. Fact is, I been thinking to pull 'em up, for then I could get me a broody hen. Can't keep any fowl now for fear they'd get into the henbane. Nothing does a chicken in faster'n henbane. And I do love fresh eggs."

Addie put a hand to her forehead, feeling bewildered.

"What about Nathan? How did he come to be that way?" She realized that the notion had become quite firmly planted in the back of her mind that Florinda had bewitched him and clouded his brain.

At the sound of his name Nathan's head came up and he looked her way. The old man explained in a soft voice, "When Caroline married Abel and came here to live she was widowed. She brought two young boys with her."

"Two!"

He nodded. "Philip — and Nathan, his younger brother. Oh, Abel had grand ideas right from the start. He wanted to rise in the world. Never had been a great success up until then, although he'd had plenty of schemes. But Nathan — well, Nathan was born different. God touched him in a special way; we don't any of us know why. But he wasn't ever the same as others. And he shamed Abel. Abel didn't want him around the house for others to see. So Nathan was sent to live with Florinda. He was a frightened, cowed thing then, with no knowledge or skills, like a little animal. But Florinda took good care of him and taught him to garden and to mend harness and fetch water and to milk — oh, dozens of things. And she fed him up and petted him a good bit, is my guess — " He glanced kindly at the would-be witch. "Till finally he grew into a good strong boy

194

able to get on fine. Oh, 'twas a lucky day for Nathan when they sent him to her. It always bothered Philip, for he felt his brother to be unfairly treated. Philip's got a good heart. But I think he sees now that it's been a good thing for Nathan."

Addie got to her feet slowly. Thoughts were revolving inside her head, shifting places and moving around until she felt dizzy with them, but one thing rose to the top and demanded attention. They were wasting time.

"What do we do now?" she asked, looking at each of them in turn, even Nathan.

"I don't know how you came to learn of all this," Jeremiah Drummond said, giving her a curious look. "But we can talk of that later. We were just taking counsel with one another when you made your entrance. Now you're here you can add your thoughts to ours."

"All we been able to do so far is talk our way in here and bolt the door," Florinda said worriedly. "I told that villain when he tried to find out more that it would take a few hours for the poison to work and I must stay right by to see that it's done proper. But that won't satisfy him for long. We got to get old Mister out of here."

"How?"

"Well — there's Nathan. He's strong enough to carry him. Strong enough to knock Abel Drummond to his last reward too, if he tries to stop us."

Old Jeremiah shook his head slowly. "Your intentions are of the best, Florinda," he said gently, "and your loyalty is most touching. But we won't make it that way, and I daresay you know it as well as I. Abel has a gun. Oh, he's not likely to use it on me, but he wouldn't hesitate to use it

195

on Nathan. Claim Nathan attacked him. No, it can't be that way."

"Then we've got to get help from the outside," Addie said desperately. "I can do it. I can sneak out and get to the village without his ever knowing. I'll get to Barker Mills and bring help."

"Who'll you go to?"

"Well — Dr. Patchett, if there's no one else."

A faint sad smile moved old Mr. Drummond's lips. "Who do you think would believe you, child? Look at us."

Addie's eyes took in the little group once more. A helpless old man, an idiot boy, and Florinda with her rusty black cape, her bent, peering stance, her gray hair sticking out in wild wisps. Addie herself, a stranger, an outsider. And balanced against them Abel Drummond, a distinguished citizen, a man of parts, an important man who knew judges and politicians.

"What about Philip?" Jeremiah Drummond asked.

"Gone to buy a horse."

"You don't know where?"

"No. Abel saw to it."

"Then there's only — "

"Yes. Jonah West. But he's at Drummondtown. And—" Addie stopped, thinking of Jonah tossing and fevered, out of his head on the straw pallet. But he might be better. Mrs. Upjohn said sometimes a fever burns out in the night. And if not — if not — Addie turned to the woman. "Florinda, can Nathan carry a message?"

"Yes indeed. Anywhere I tell him. For all his mind's like a child's, he knows the fields and woods and every road and trail. He's at home under the sky, Nathan is."

196

"Can we sneak him out of the house?"

"I can say he's underfoot and I want him back home."

"Then I'll need pen and paper. We must get a message out. And if help doesn't come by morning, you must delay some way, Florinda. We may need a few more hours."

"I'll try to think of something," Florinda muttered.

The hours crept slowly on toward midnight. Florinda nodded off and then woke jerkily, wrapped in her cloak in the big chair by the bed. Addie paced up and down, pausing time and again in front of the window to look out at nothing. There was no help on the empty horizon, yet she felt compelled to keep looking. She knew Rose-Anne must be sleepless and anxious in their own room; still she felt she could not leave yet. How long had Nathan been gone? Two hours? How many hours till dawn? Not nearly enough. Not nearly.

"Sit down, child. Sit down and rest," the old man whispered, watching her restless movements.

"I'm sorry. I'm keeping you awake. *You* should rest," she apologized.

"No need, no need." He waved the idea away. He went on softly, "But there is something I've been wondering."

She approached the bed noiselessly in her soft slippers and stood there for a moment looking down at him. In the moving candlelight his eyes were narrowed and searching as they looked at her, studying her face earnestly.

"Have you been wondering who I am?" she whispered.

Rather unexpectedly he smiled. "Oh, no. Not that. I've known for some time who you are."

Addie did not answer, feeling quavery and uncertain. He

went on, "Oh, certainly. Your nose, your sister's eyes. And so many things. A way of moving a hand, a step, a gesture — those are the ways the blood shows itself. I'd have known you both — anywhere."

"But you never let on!"

"It's hard to explain," he said, thinking about it, and now Addie dropped down and sat on the edge of the bed, taking his hand in both of hers. "When my Carlotta died — your mother — this illness struck me. And I knew it was a judgment on me. It was the hand of God. A punishment for my wicked stubbornness. I'd never forgiven her, you see, for marrying — well, no matter about that. But then you and your sister came here, and it almost seemed — I almost believed I was being offered a second chance. A way to make it up to you and, through you, to my daughter. I guessed you might have been left alone in the world and that that was why you were here."

"Yes, that was true," Addie said. "We had lost our father."

"But you made no move to introduce yourselves and I pondered why. Did you hate me so much? It might be, I thought, yet you seemed to want to help me, and you were such gentle, tender girls. Still I was afraid to speak out for fear of saying the wrong thing. I've done a great deal of that in my time — "

"I only feared for your health, Grandfather," Addie said earnestly. "So many times I wanted to tell you! But perhaps I was afraid of other things too."

"Yes, yes, just so," he agreed. "We were strangers, one to the other, and wary."

Florinda, hunched in the chair, opened one eye and listened with interest.

"But what did you mean?" Addie asked. "What did you mean a minute ago when you said you were wondering about something? What was it then that you wondered?"

Old Jeremiah's brows came together in a frown as if he were studying on something. He looked from her to the window.

"How in the devil," he said, "did you get around to that window?"

"I walked the cornice, up above on the roof."

"Walked the cornice!"

"It's a skill I have," Addie said, hoping it did not sound too proud. She saw the amazement in his face and realization came to her that for all they had gotten acquainted in this hour of fear and danger, something still was not open, not right between them. She knew what it was and knew too that it must be brought into the light. So she added, "It's a skill my father taught me."

His expression did not change. He seemed not to have heard, yet Addie knew that he was too sharp for that. He shook his head as though finding it hard to believe and said, "The Lord must surely have been looking out for you, my dear."

"I'm sure He was. I felt my father's help as well."

"It was a brave thing to do."

"I learned that too from my father," Addie said stubbornly.

Old Jeremiah looked down at the coverlet, keeping his eyes averted for a long time. Finally he raised them to her and said simply, "Perhaps I have misjudged your father then. Perhaps — he was a man I would have liked."

Addie had not realized she was holding her breath, but now it came out in a rush. She answered, "I'm sure you would have, Grandfather. I'm sure he'd have liked you too." His saying that, she thought, must have taken nearly as much courage as her finding her footing on the roof.

19

Florinda slipped the latch and let her out before dawn and she made her way on silent feet back to the room she shared with Rose-Anne. Rose-Anne had not undressed all night.

"Didn't you sleep?" Addie asked.

"I napped a little. But I kept listening for you. What about Grandfather? Is he all right?"

"Yes, so far." And Addie explained to her Florinda's delaying action and Nathan's going for help. Rose-Anne listened, nodding and putting in questions, wanting to understand it all. As Addie finished, her mouth turned down slightly.

"It's a little disappointing, isn't it? I mean — in a way. It would have been nice if she'd been a real witch."

Addie was pulling off the middy and trousers, changing back into her dress. "I don't care what she is just so she's on our side."

"But how long can she make excuses to Abel? He's going to be impatient, isn't he?"

"Well, then we must help. We must do our part the very best we can. Nothing to make him nervous. You know — as if we suspect nothing at all. Everything as normal as we can make it."

They tidied themselves, put on fresh aprons and scrubbed their faces hard in cold water to bring some color in place of the sleepless pallor.

"There. I guess that's the best we can do," Rose-Anne observed doubtfully.

"It'll do. He won't be thinking about us anyway."

"You don't think he suspects us at all?"

"I don't think so. And I know he doesn't suspect Florinda. He gave her two gold coins."

"Gold eagles?" Rose-Anne's eyes widened.

"Yes. Twenty dollars. I'm sure he feels that was enough to buy her skill and her loyalty too."

"How little he knows about loyalty," Rose-Anne murmured.

At the door Addie paused and said, "Rose-Anne, he knows who we are. Our grandfather knows."

"He does!"

"Yes, and he's pleased. He likes us."

Rose-Anne created a breakfast of heroic proportions. Plump fried sausages that spurted juice when stuck with a fork, eggs, biscuits, preserves. She served it on a blue and white tablecloth in the kitchen and even placed a pitcher of black-eyed Susans in the center of the table.

"There now, Cousin Abel, sit right down and enjoy it,"

she said warmly when he entered. "I'll bet you don't eat well at all traveling about as much as you do. And I want you to give a good report of me to Mrs. Upjohn when she returns."

He glanced from her to Addie, a cautious, probing look. His face showed weariness and lines as though he too had slept poorly. Yet his eyes were sharp and bright with elation, the only thing about him to betray excitement.

"Yes, do, Cousin Abel," Addie chimed in. "And I'll fetch more butter from the spring house if you need it."

"Perhaps I'd better go out to the barn first," Abel said, "to see if Nathan is at his chores."

"Oh, he is. I saw him not a moment ago," Addie assured him, hoping no cow would start bawling for want of milking. "And indeed he does seem surprisingly capable, as you said."

"Well, then, perhaps it can wait until later," Abel conceded. "That does look delicious, my dear."

"Addie, run up with Grandfather's tray, will you?" Rose-Anne said, but Abel, who had started to take a seat at the table, whirled around.

"Please allow me," he said.

The moment hung tensely and then Addie said, "Oh, very well," and thanked him with a smile. "Some days it does seem I count five hundred of those stairs."

When he was gone, Rose-Anne turned to her in desperation. "Why did you let him take it?"

"I couldn't have stopped him, could I? And it would only have made him suspicious. I'm going part way up the backstairs to see if I can hear anything."

"Be careful!"

Addie tiptoed up the stairs from the kitchen, pausing near the top and listening hard. A door opened and closed and there was silence for a moment. Then it opened and closed again, and now she could hear voices in the hall above. They were low and she had to strain to hear.

"What do you mean — longer?"

"Why, sir, as I explained. Because to work its way properly through the blood takes time."

"It should have been over by now. You said it would be."

"I named no hour. And you see yourself how he looks. No sign of life. No awakening."

"But breathing still."

"Ah, yes, but breath is the last to flee the body. His heart's beating is near done."

"Well, you're not needed any longer. Go along home."

"It's important that I stand by and keep watch."

"It's not important at all." Abel's voice was curt now, master to servant. "Be off with you at once. I can manage the thing myself from here on."

"Oh, sir, I doubt the wisdom of that — "

"You heard me. Downstairs at once and straight home. And not a word to anyone. I'll know how to deal with you and the boy if there's any talk."

"Be sure not to touch him or disturb what I've set in motion."

Their footsteps drew nearer and Addie turned and fled back to the kitchen.

"He's sending Florinda away," she gasped, and there was just time for them to arrange their expressions before Abel and Florinda came in. The two girls managed to look properly startled at seeing the old woman.

"Be on your way now, Florinda," Abel said kindly. "I'm sure your draught will act as a restorative to him. I called Florinda in last evening," he explained, "when it seemed to me Uncle looked weak and poorly. She has a good knowledge of medicines and herbs. Of course I shall summon Dr. Patchett to bleed him today if he shows no improvement."

Addie looked properly troubled. "Indeed! I had no notion our grandfather was unwell. Perhaps I should go sit with him."

"Not at all. Have your breakfast, my dear. He's resting quite comfortably at the moment. Later I shall sit with him myself for a time. It may be that he has exceeded his strength in some way — oh, not that I blame you one bit. But walking, getting about — these may have stimulated the blood to a dangerous level. One can't be sure." He turned to Florinda. "Get along now, woman," he told her briskly as she stood there hesitating and looking with longing at the eggs. And with no more argument she slid out through the back door, her ragged cloak drawn around her. There was no chance for a sign or a look from her to either of the girls.

Abel watched her go before turning back to the table, and something in his expression seemed to lighten as though with relief or the lifting of anxiety. He looked with pleasure at the plate of food Rose-Anne had placed on the table and rubbed his hands together.

"Now, then. Let me appreciate your new skills, my

dear," he said to Rose-Anne. "I seem to have more appetite than I thought."

He said nothing more about going to the barn after breakfast. He seemed to be taking Addie's word for Nathan's presence. Instead he headed for the dining room where he often worked when he was at home, and presently they could hear him moving papers about, scratching with his pen and whistling softly. Addie and Rose-Anne kept busy in the kitchen, chatting in a normal way. Once out of the window they spied Florinda scuttling about up at the barn and guessed that she was doing the chores and the milking.

The day dragged along sluggishly. The sun seemed to climb with an indifferent slowness. Each hour doubled and tripled its length. When Rose-Anne suggested that it was time for the noon meal there was no interest, even from Abel, who protested when she stepped to the door of the dining room that he had eaten heartily enough of her fine breakfast to last him until sundown or near to it. "I think it might be wise to wait with your grandfather's tray too," he said thoughtfully. "Right now he needs rest more than food."

"He's giving it plenty of time," Rose-Anne whispered, coming back to the kitchen.

"Yes. He hopes to go up and find Grandfather dead and then come rushing down to tell us."

"But when he goes up and finds him *not* dead — Addie, it wouldn't take much. You know, for him to do it himself. Just a pillow over an old man's face — "

"We can't let him go up there again, that's all."

206

"How can we stop him?"

"I have to think!" Addie did not tell Rose-Anne about the gun, but she knew Abel would not hesitate to use it. As a last resort he would. There was always Nathan, who could be blamed.

"Addie, do you think Nathan's had time to get there? Do you think — "

"I don't know! Let's just concentrate on keeping Abel downstairs."

But shortly after midday they could tell he was growing restless. He forsook his work at the dining room table and began to walk about from room to room. Several times he paced up and down the front hall and Addie, who had come out with her dustcloth and was making a large fuss over dusting, saw him glance first at the hall clock and then at the stairs. She engaged him at once in conversation, desperately dredging up questions and topics. Did he surmise Philip had had any luck in finding a suitable horse? What was his guess as to the ailment that had befallen the horse that died? She did hope the Philadelphia weather would prove pleasant for Cousin Caroline's visit. Of course late summer could be chancy in the city. There was that year of the great yellow fever plague — But of course nowadays one didn't hear much of that sort of thing. Noxious vapors from the swampland, some said, had been the cause of it, but one could not be sure —

He answered her in monosyllables and kept looking at the stairs. And all at once he said decisively, "Excuse me, my dear, I think perhaps I'd best look in on Uncle Jeremiah."

And he started up the stairs.

For a heart's beat Addie stood there frozen. Then she

called after him, "Before you go, Cousin Abel — " And saw him pause and turn halfway up the stairs.

"Yes, what is it?" He sounded annoyed.

And Addie knew quite suddenly that they were lost. That this was the moment, and that there was no help, that there was no more she could do except to throw herself upon Abel Drummond, biting and scratching, and even that might not work, for there was the gun. Perhaps a small gun around which, even now, his hand might be closing in the pocket of his well-tailored coat.

"I only wanted to ask you — " she stammered, when a sound from outside sent her flying to the front window. "Cousin Abel! Someone's here! A carriage is stopping at the front steps!"

Abel frowned. "Who is it?" He started back down the stairs.

Addie turned to him with a bewildered look. "I can't tell. But it's a very stylish carriage and a man's getting out."

Abel hurried to join her at the window. "Good Lord! That's got to be Vreeland."

"Who?"

"A man I've been expecting from back East. And Madam's with him. Great heavens, I never thought — Addie, we'll want a tea tray. And please. Something fine. Caroline's Boston silver. Do it very nicely. No, wait. Let them in first. Hide that dust rag and open the door. I'll wait in the parlor."

20

THE VREELANDS, husband and wife, entered the house like square-riggers under full canvas — slowly and with heavy dignity. Madam's eyes, passing over Addie with indifference, narrowed slightly to peer around the house, appraising the furnishings. The two were warmly dressed for the summer day, Mrs. Vreeland in heavy peach satin, her husband in black broadcloth with fine linen and polished boots. Everything they wore was eastern and stylish and both looked as if they dined habitually on roast goose, suet pudding and syllabub. The straining of seams was all but audible.

Abel came out of the parlor gracefully, a picture of delighted surprise. "I thought I heard — " he began. And then, charmingly, "Why — can this possibly — "

"Jan Vreeland, at your service," the man said. "Mr. Abel Drummond?"

"Yes — yes, indeed. And this must be — "

"My wife, yes."

Abel bowed low over Mrs. Vreeland's hand and then shook Mr. Vreeland's. Addie marveled at the way he managed to combine poise with exactly the right measure of deference.

"What excellent time you made coming westward!" he exclaimed. "I hardly dared expect you so soon."

"Ah, yes. We came in our own carriage and with a capable driver," Mr. Vreeland explained. "Faster than by stage."

"Roads were abominable, however," Mrs. Vreeland added glumly.

They both spoke with the heavy Dutch accents of the Hudson valley, and Madam managed to convey a general disapproval of all existence west of Albany.

"Well! Come in, come in!" Abel urged. "I do regret that Mrs. Drummond — my wife — is on a visit to Philadelphia. She will be most unhappy to have missed you. Ladies of refinement are never numerous enough here to satisfy her desire for companionship."

Mrs. Vreeland's expression gave no sign that she was experiencing similar disappointment.

"Adelina," Abel ordered her, "a tea tray, please." And Addie, slipping into character, dropped a curtsy and hurried back toward the kitchen.

"May we see to your horse?" Abel's voice followed her out.

"No, no. My man will take care of it."

"Well, then, do take a seat please, and make yourselves comfortable. You have lodgings in the village?"

"We do, yes. Arrived last night."

Mrs. Vreeland made some comment that Addie did not catch, but it had a petulant sound as though she found the local accommodations less than adequate. Addie ducked into the kitchen and found Rose-Anne already setting up a tea tray with Caroline's good silver and the best china.

"I was listening at the door," she whispered, and Addie could see that her hands trembled slightly so that the cups clinked together. "He was starting upstairs, wasn't he?"

"Yes." And now Addie noticed that Mrs. Upjohn's heavy wooden potato masher was on the table by the tea tray. Rose-Anne must have been holding it as she listened at the door.

"We can't wait any longer," Addie said, finding that her fear had been supplanted, rather unexpectedly, by clarity and businesslike purpose. "When I take the tea tray in, go up to Grandfather's room and tell him to dress quickly. Then come down and go to the pasture for General Strong. Florinda's probably out there. She can help you saddle him. Bring him around to the back door here. You and Grandfather will have to leave together — he can't go alone — but the General can carry you both. It's only three miles to the village. Go straight to the inn and sit at a table in the public room where people can see you and wait for me. I'll follow on foot; it won't take me long."

"Are you sure you can get away?"

"Of course. I'll leave when you do."

"All right." Rose-Anne was pale as she went to the crane for the teakettle.

The tea tray, when Addie brought it, looked elegant. Caroline's silver teapot gleamed and steamed, its dull rich finish beautifully polished by Rose-Anne. The translucent china cups had tiny violets and roses painted on them and the silver spoons were wafer-thin and graceful. Mrs. Vreeland stared openly as Addie carried it in, and lifted one of the cups before the tea was poured to examine the bottom of it. Jan Vreeland was talking expansively.

" — other investments in western land, of course, but this sounded to me like something my partners and I might take an interest in. There's a group of us — you probably know the names — van Schoyk, Albemeer, van Renssalaer — but we're all easterners. You're right out here where the thing is building. What we have in mind is to combine resources, you see. It could be to your advantage as well as ours."

"Yes, yes, I see your meaning," Abel replied lightly, not showing too great an interest at first. "Roads and mail routes are a first consideration, of course, and I've been devoting attention to those. The town itself is a going thing by now."

"Of course it's no secret either that it would be helpful to a group like ours to have a man in the state legislature. Even governor, when it comes to that, and it seems to me you might be a good candidate, Drummond."

Mrs. Vreeland sipped at her tea and devoured one of Rose-Anne's little spice cakes in two bites.

"Of course title and ownership will have to be worked out," Vreeland continued. "I assume you are the sole owner of these holdings?"

Abel did not hesitate. "Oh, yes. Yes, of course."

"And with a town established, it seems to me the entire surrounding territory would be ripe for settlement."

"I think there can be no question of that. And it might be that with a fresh infusion of capital — "

Addie finished pouring and tiptoed out dutifully. Once in the kitchen she glanced out the back door and saw Rose-Anne running toward the pasture, skirts held up over her knees. Addie hurried to the backstairs and climbed them silently.

In spite of her haste she stopped and stared in astonishment when she pushed open the door of her grandfather's room. She had grown so accustomed to the sight of him as an invalid, pale and bent in his nightgown and shawl, that seeing him up and dressed, seated in the chair, was like coming in unexpectedly on a stranger. He sat there with his back straighter than usual, both hands, slender and white, resting on the arms of the chair. He looked surprisingly handsome and dignified.

"Grandfather, how fine you look!" Addie whispered. "You got ready so quickly too."

"I thought I'd best be prepared for anything," he admitted. "I've been dressed for two hours."

"Rose-Anne told you the plan?"

He nodded. "My horsemanship may not be of the best these days, but I daresay I can hang on."

"There are the steps too," Addie said doubtfully. "You haven't tried any steps yet, but — "

"I shall manage," he said firmly, and got up.

She walked ahead of him down the stairs, looking back anxiously over her shoulder, but he did well enough, hanging on to the railing and taking a step at a time, bringing both feet together before trying the next one. It was a slow descent, but Addie could still hear the voices coming from the front parlor. By the time they made it to the back door, she could see Rose-Anne coming down the slope leading General Strong by the bridle. She brought him around to the doorstep and held him there.

"You first," Addie told Rose-Anne. "I'll steady him."

Rose-Anne mounted lightly onto the General's back, then eased forward and took her feet out of the stirrups so that old Jeremiah could slip his foot in. He did so, but then was stopped; he could go no further. The weakened muscles, which had carried him bravely down the steps, simply refused this last effort. The General's back looked suddenly, like Mercutio's wound, not so wide as a church door, but impossibly high, impossibly out of reach. Addie saw it and felt panic rise inside her in a hot wave.

"Oh, God, please help us!" she burst out frantically.

Then Rose-Anne leaned forward, clutching the General's mane, and spoke into his ear. "Bow to the crowd, General!" she ordered. "Bow to the crowd!"

Slowly, elegantly, General Strong bent his two front legs and lowered his head modestly before the unseen audience. The inches gained were just enough so that Addie, with a mighty push, could hoist the old man into the saddle. And at the same moment she heard Abel calling her from inside the house.

She and Rose-Anne exchanged one bleak terrified look. "Addie! Don't go back in!"

Addie shook her head, thinking fast. "Only for a minute," she said. "Then I'll sneak out and follow after you."

"Addie — no — "

"Go, General!" Addie ordered him, and slapped his

rump. "Hold on, Grandfather!" And the General did his little prancing step and then trotted off gracefully down the lane toward the road. She could see Rose-Anne's white face looking back toward her, and then she turned and went in through the kitchen door. Abel Drummond stood there framed in the doorway from the hall. He was frowning.

"What's going on here?" There was no friendliness in his voice now, no more pretense. He spoke as he had spoken to Florinda, master to servant. "I heard a horse."

"The traveling tinker was at the back door, Cousin Abel," Addie said. "He wanted to mend pots. I sent him away since you had guests and we were busy."

His eyes looked cold and searching. The lids had a half-closed, suspicious look. He scanned the kitchen. "Where is your sister?"

"Out at the barn gathering eggs."

He seemed to accept this and went on, "Madam desires more tea. Please brew a fresh pot."

"Very well. I'll come and fetch the tray."

Abel turned to go back to the parlor and Addie followed after. She should have ducked out and fled when Rose-Anne and her grandfather had. But then Abel might have glimpsed the horse and known what was afoot. She had had to give them those extra few minutes to get away. But she was still safe as long as she was not alone in the house with him. That was all she had to fear. And if, she thought as an idea occurred to her, she was to be treated as a country servant girl, perhaps she would do well to act more like one. As she re-entered the parlor behind Abel she made her step less lively, more reluctant. Her bright and willing face turned surly and she wiped her nose on the corner of her apron.

"Now quickly, if you please," Abel ordered her sharply, and he readjusted his expression to cordiality as he seated himself once more with the Vreelands. The tray lay in ruins, demolished and crumb-laden. Addie stared at it sourly and then mumbled, "Are you sure there's naught left in the pot?"

Abel glared at her with astonishment. "I said we want fresh. Kindly fetch it at once, Miss."

Addie picked up the silver teapot as if to test the truth of the matter, sloshed it around and then gave it a slight tilt which sent tea slopping into Madam's peach satin lap. The woman rose, a heaving fury.

"You stupid girl!" she roared. "Look what you've done!"

"Adelina! This is inexcusable!" Abel had risen too, white with anger.

"It wants only sponging, Madam," Addie said with a scowl. "It's naught but a little tea."

"Well, who's to do it?" the woman shrieked. "I'm traveling without a maid and those fools at the inn — "

Mr. Vreeland fidgeted nervously. "Perhaps we'd best leave then and resume our talk tomorrow," he said in the fussy anxious way of men when a quarrel between women looms. He drew a fine linen handkerchief from his sleeve and made a few passes at the spreading stain. Madam struck his hand away. Suddenly an idea seemed to occur to him. "But if you would permit your girl here to come along with us to the inn — uh — to assist Madam — uh, just for an hour or two — "

216

"By all means. Certainly. Adelina, go with the Vreelands and stay as long as Madam needs your services. Inexcusable! Madam, my most abject apologies. Sir, I cannot express my regret strongly enough."

Mr. Vreeland made small placating motions of his hands behind his wife's back and cast Abel a look that was almost comradely as Mrs. Vreeland, swaying grandly from side to side in her outrage, stalked out. Addie followed after with set, glum face and Mr. Vreeland brought up the rear.

Addie sat straight and tight-lipped in the stylish carriage beside Mrs. Vreeland. Mr. Vreeland, opposite them, settled back with a sigh and consulted his gold watch. He bowed to Abel as they pulled away and lifted a hand in farewell. Up front the driver clucked at the horses and jiggled the reins and they moved off slowly down the drive toward the road. For several minutes the three inside the carriage sat silently, all of them looking back toward the house until Abel Drummond was a small faraway figure and they were on the road headed toward the village. Only then did the mood in the carriage alter in a slow subtle way. It happened to Madam first. The end of her nose turned red and her eyes filled with tears which spilled down her cheeks in two streams. Mr. Vreeland cleared his throat loudly. Addie swallowed and then swallowed again with a loud lumpy sound but it did not help. She was crying herself by now.

"Maybelle," she whispered, sobbing. "Maybelle, you were great." She leaned against Maybelle's round bosom with a sudden weariness, at the same time reaching out with one hand. "Billy — dear Billy." She seized his hand. "You were wonderful. Simply splendid. You couldn't have been better — both of you."

"Oh, now, fiddle, dear. It was no great thing," Billy said lightly. "A replay of *Rake's Revenge*. Maybelle and I both recognized the plot as soon as we read your letter. Of course it's been some time since we played it and I'm rusty at straight parts myself."

"We were just a tiny bit nervous too, when we got your message, because of that strange boy who brought it," Maybelle said. "But as Billy said, if Addie trusts him then we must trust him too."

"Oh, I knew you would come if there was any way to. It was all I could think of because I knew Dingman's Grove was where you were playing, and I knew it wasn't far off. But wherever did you get this elegant carriage?"

"You don't recognize it?" Billy asked. "Belongs to Mrs. Millhaus — the old dragon herself. When I asked her for the loan of it and told her your predicament, she came through handsomely and insisted we take it. Abner volunteered to act as coachman; he said it would be a stimulating change from fiddling."

"Oh, bless his heart — yes, I saw him. I shall thank him properly when we're away from here."

"And Rose-Anne — and your grandfather? They're safe?" Maybelle asked.

"Yes, they got away. They'll be waiting for us in the village."

Maybelle wiped her eyes and blew her nose. "I had just one bad moment," she confessed. "When you spilled that tea I was dumfounded, for you hadn't given me any cue for

218

it. Of course I knew you'd done it on purpose, for you'd never make such a mess of a simple bit of stage business. Something's amiss, I said, but play it straight, Maybelle, play it for logic."

"I was sure you would. And Billy picked up the cue beautifully. I'd told you in the note to stay for a few minutes and leave naturally, but then I was afraid to have you leave for fear I wouldn't be able to get away myself. That was when I thought of spilling the tea."

"Oh, splendid improvisation, dear. Splendid."

"But that's your best dress, the one you wear for your closing number. I do hope we can clean it up."

"Nonsense. Small matter. Oh, love, how good it is to see you again!"

They rode along for a few minutes in warm companionable silence, depleted by emotion. Then Billy began to smile to himself in a self-satisfied way.

"Carried it off right enough, didn't we?" he mused. "You know, I wouldn't have thought I was up to a straight part any more after all this time." He grew a trifle pompous. "Makes one wonder if one should confine oneself entirely to comedy if one still has the — ah — resources for this sort of thing. I shall have trouble getting back to my fox in the henhouse routine tonight, I fear. After working on a higher dramatic level, that is."

Addie smiled at him and patted his hand. Then she grew thoughtful. "I suppose we could have managed him if it had come to that, couldn't we?" She considered it. "I mean the three of us. We could have whacked him over the head or tied him up or something."

"Ah, but one never knows," Billy countered with a raised

finger. "One can't tell what view the authorities would take. Maybelle and I were there as impostors, after all. And besides, this had so much more — style."

21

THE TWO CHICKENS had been dispatched and plucked almost before Addie was aware of it and now they cooked juicily over the built-up fire in the kitchen. With a true appreciation of first things first, Mrs. Upjohn had started to prepare food the minute her foot stepped over the threshold. Small potatoes were roasting on the hob, beans were simmering in an iron pot on the crane, and something was baking and bubbling between crusts in the oven. The kitchen was crowded, but there were no complaints from Mrs. Upjohn about people being underfoot.

Old Jeremiah Drummond sat at one end of the table, a little flushed with excitement, his eyes following Addie and Rose-Anne as they moved about. Jonah West sat on one side of him, Philip Hess on the other.

"But what about Abel?" Jonah was saying urgently. "He got away then?"

"Yes. No surprise really. He knew the game was up. He was gone when the girls and I got back."

"He should be followed and brought here," Jonah said angrily. "He should be held for the law. Where will he head, do you think?"

"Oh, probably Philadelphia. Caroline has kin there. Maybe he'll take ship to England even. Yes, yes, I know he should be held for the law," the old man agreed with a troubled look, "yet in spite of all I could take no satisfaction in that. He is after all family. And there's Philip's mother, who is quite innocent. I wouldn't want her hurt. And out of it all I've gained more than I've lost," he added, looking at his two granddaughters.

They had known even before they re-entered the house that they would find it empty. Addie and Rose-Anne had returned with their grandfather, along with Eleazar Bates, the local captain of militia, and Judge Hampton Perry. Both men had been astounded at seeing their old friend hale and well, sitting ramrod-straight in the public room of the Barker Mills tavern, and both had been incredulous at the account of Abel's perfidy. Neither man had for a moment doubted old Jeremiah's word, and it amazed Addie how quickly he was able to assume a commanding air and to take charge of the situation. They had said farewell to Billy, Maybelle and Abner at the tavern with many embraces, handshakes and promises to meet again. Jeremiah Drummond had thanked the three over and over and had listened several times to an account of the scene with Abel. He had insisted that they must pay a real visit soon.

"Those friends of yours are splendid," he had said, shaking his head in wonder at the whole affair and waving them down the road and out of sight as they departed for

Dingman's Grove. "I'd have liked to see more of them."

"They have a performance tonight," Addie explained. "They had to hurry back."

"Ah, yes. Just so. An obligation," he agreed, understanding. "But I must see them again nevertheless. Such friends are rare."

And so they had returned to the farm and to the deserted house where they found doors left ajar and a rug askew as though caught by hastening feet, the tea tray in the parlor with dregs still in the china cups, and the whole house wide and empty.

First to return after that was Philip, who had come through Barker Mills not long after they had left it and who had heard the news there and ridden the three miles home at top speed. Rose-Anne, hearing hoofbeats in the dooryard, had run outside to meet him, and Addie had passed the open door just in time to see Philip leap off his horse and Rose-Anne run to his arms. Not long afterward Jonah and Mrs. Upjohn had come careening along in Caroline's light rig, the whole affair tilting recklessly, Mrs. Upjohn clutching her reticule, her bonnet hanging over one ear.

"He didn't no more than come back to his wits after that fever before he said we'd have to get right back here," she explained. And indeed Jonah did look hollow-eyed, unshaven, pale. Addie did not run to him as Rose-Anne had run to Philip. She stood clutching her two hands together under her apron as his eyes picked her out and he asked anxiously, "Addie — are you all right?"

"I'm fine, yes," she said. But she felt his eyes on her for a long time even after she had looked away.

As the cooking smells thickened, Florinda and Nathan appeared at the back door and were invited in. Florinda entered willingly and sat down at once at the table but Nathan was shy of the crowd and hung back. Mrs. Upjohn filled a plate for him and let him sit on the back step and eat by himself. Later Addie saw that he had walked up the slope to the pasture fence, and that he and General Strong were standing there with their heads close together.

"You could do with some rest yourself," Jeremiah Drummond was saying to Jonah as Addie brought her attention back to the table. "Come to me tomorrow and we'll discuss business. I want to know exactly how things stand at the town site. Addie has told me enough of the situation so that I know we must start from the ground up. I already have some thoughts on the matter. Philip, I'll want to talk to you too. Perhaps we could use some of the Germans here to help with the harvest — that young man Addie spoke of for one, and perhaps some others. A few of them might winter here on the farm. Jonah, you could move in here at the main house and we could use the small house for one or two families. Then some can go to the Quaker settlement with the agreement to return in the spring."

Jonah and Philip, listening on either side of him, nodded agreement.

"We should see about getting a mill built as soon as possible," the old man went on. "There's plenty of timber there, and if we could have cut lumber for our building everything would progress at a faster rate. Besides — "

"Grandfather," Addie interrupted. "Tomorrow's time enough. If you're finished eating, perhaps I should help you to your room now."

Jonah glanced at her. "I think you'd better go, sir. She has a way of managing things."

"Ah, yes. Well, tomorrow then," Jeremiah agreed, and he left the kitchen, leaning on his cane and holding Addie's arm, but still looking surprisingly hale.

After Addie had seen him to his room she did not return at once to the kitchen, but went down the hall to her own room and stepped inside. She could hear the voices coming from below in the kitchen where they all sat, lingering, talking, wearing out the day with recollection and wonder. Through the window she could see late sunlight and long shadows that were already showing the faint lavender of the August evening coming on. The dry worn look of a season spent lay over everything. She felt that way herself, Addie reflected, although that was perhaps only because she had not slept since night before last. And oddly, she was still not sleepy; she felt light and rather empty and her feet seemed not quite to touch the floor when she walked. Yet sleep was not what she wanted — not yet.

She crossed the room and picked up the sailor trousers and middy which still lay in a heap on the floor. She carried them to the bed and then pulled from under it her old traveling bag. She folded the things and put them away, and it was then that the door opened and Rose-Anne came in. Her eyes went to the bag.

"Addie! What are you doing?"

"Just putting things away."

"But why in your traveling bag?"

Addie shrugged. "It'll soon be time to leave. I thought I might as well."

Rose-Anne looked troubled. "Addie — there's something I must talk to you about. I know how you've been counting on the two of us working up a new act for the season — going back to Philadelphia. I just can't. I'm not going back."

Addie raised her eyes from the bag.

"I'm staying here on the farm, Addie. I'm going to marry Philip."

Addie nodded. "I know."

"I feel I belong here," Rose-Anne went on. "And with Philip. But I know you'll do well by yourself. You're so talented, Addie."

Addie nodded again, not arguing the point.

"Unless — " A new idea struck Rose-Anne. "Unless you'd consider staying too. Would you? Grandfather would be so pleased."

Addie shook her head. "I'll come and visit; I surely will. But I have to go back to Philadelphia. I have to try my luck first."

"You're not angry with me?" There were tears in Rose-Anne's eyes and Addie went to her quickly and hugged her.

"Oh, Rose-Anne, how silly you are. I know you belong here too. I suppose I knew it right along. And it will make me happy thinking you're here looking out for Grandfather. Go along down to Philip now."

"Aren't you coming?"

"In a minute."

She waited after Rose-Anne left and then went out into the hall and down the front steps instead of the back ones that led to the kitchen. Quietly she slipped out the door and circled the house to the back, heading for General Strong's pasture.

She found Nathan still there by the fence stroking the General's forehead. He shrank back fearfully when he saw her approaching, and she remembered how she had shouted and thrown a stone at him last time she had caught him there. This time she smiled and spoke his name and talked with him in a quiet voice for a time, telling him what a performing wonder the General was and finally taking his hand in hers and placing it on the horse's neck. She left the two of them there after a few moments and walked back slowly toward the house. Darkness was moving in fast now, and she saw that candles had been lighted in the kitchen. Fireflies were out, moving and winking among the shadows. As she approached the house, someone stepped out of the darkness. It was Jonah.

"Addie — is everything all right?"

"Yes. I went to see my horse and to make my peace with Nathan. I haven't been very nice to him."

"Your sister says you'll be leaving soon."

"I will, yes."

"Your grandfather will be disappointed."

"No. Grandfather will understand. Once he might not have, but now he will. And I'll come back to visit."

"Addie, why don't you stay? It would mean so much to all of us — to me especially."

Something came over Addie, an odd feeling that was new to her. Not weariness or excitement or fear or anything she had ever felt before. A warm feeling that stirred and moved within her so strongly that she felt a trembling start up in her legs. She made a wavering, uncertain move and he caught her by the arm.

"Oh la, sir," she said, imitating Florinda, "I be no proper country girl. I must go back to the city — to the theater, where I belong." She was very much aware of his hand supporting her.

"And what if you find, once you get there, that it isn't where you belong after all?"

"How could it not be? It's what I do!"

"What if I were to come to Philadelphia then, to see you perform? And what if I were to ask you to come back here? To marry me?"

Addie gave a startled gasp and for a moment was unable to speak. Marry Jonah? Had he really said that? She collected herself and tried to frame an answer, but no answer came because she could not, at this moment, find one within herself. How could she tell whether she would miss the plowed fields, the slope of hills, the voice of the wind, the smell of morning in the country? How could she know whether she would miss Jonah West in a way that might be unlike any missing she had ever known?

"If you come to Philadelphia I should be most happy, of course," she said, and then she thought, how prim I sound. How like a brown mouse soberly cracking a seed, neat and proper. "Oh Jonah," she burst out, "do come to Philadelphia! I want you to come!"

His head tipped back and he laughed, and then his arm came around her and they began walking back to the house together.

In the little burying ground the stone stood out from those around it. Because it was newer than the rest it stood straight and untilted and there was no hint of moss or weathering about it. There were weeds, however, and Addie pulled them, leaving only some wild chicory and Queen Anne's lace because she thought they decorated the grave nicely. Then she dropped down on her knees and lingered awhile, putting a finger out to trace the letters on the stone, remarking to herself that the stonecutter had done a neat job. She would stop at his house on her way along the road and give him his final payment.

"The summer worked out fine, Papa," she said softly. "We're going to be all right, Rose-Anne and I." And she wept a little, kneeling there, because she had not wept when Terence died.

Later, when she had paid the stonecutter, she got back on her horse and started eastward on the road that led to Philadelphia. It was her last tie to the summer, paying that debt. Now it lay behind her, all of it, spread out in the sun like a tapestry or like one of Bowen's Great Emblematical Transparent Paintings that he used as backdrop for a Patriotic Historical Scene. Still, for all that had happened, she was the same Addie Trimble, she thought. The only one of the Four Dancing Trimbles left to the theater, but that was no matter — she would make her way.

Papa and Mama are together again, she thought, and Rose-Anne is with Philip where she belongs. I have a grandfather I never had before; things will work out. I'm the same me as ever. Or am I? How silly to say that really. I'm not the same at all. Anything that touches our lives affects us, changes us in some way. How could I not be different after all that has happened? How could I not be different after knowing Jonah West?

It was Jonah she thought of most as she rode along listening to the General's hooves clopping on the hard-packed dirt of the road; Jonah's face that stayed with her and his voice. But then another thought pushed in, teasing and nagging. A memory really. That first morning on the farm, the morning she had gone to Florinda's little house in the meadow. It had all been an act, of course. She realized it now. The charms, the magic, the potions, the hollow voice calling up sorcery. But there had been that fire that had sprung to life in the cold fireplace at a look from Florinda. Addie knew that had happened for she had seen it. How on earth had the woman managed it?

She shook her head and frowned as she puzzled on it, but then at last she sighed and gave General Strong a gentle nudge with her heels. Ah, well, no matter. Every good act had its tricks, she supposed.